Christmas Crosswords

Phil Clarke

Illustrated by the Pope Twins

Designed by Michael Hill

Edited by Sam Taplin

How to solve crosswords

The crosswords in this book start off simple and gradually get harder. If you're new to crosswords, here are a few tips.

It's a good idea to use a pencil with an eraser or to write lightly with a pen so that you can remove or write over mistakes.

There are two lists of clues: one for answers that read across the crossword grid, and one for those that read down.

Start wherever you like. If you can't solve one clue, move onto another that crosses it. The letters from that answer will help you. For example, solving the down answers below gives you B_A_D for 7 across, leading you towards the answer: BEARD.

ACROSS

1. Neck-warmer (5)
4. Circular (5)
7. Santa's is long and white (5)

DOWN

2. The sound doves make (3)
3. Short for Ronald (3)
4. Chest bone (3)
5. America (1.1.1.)
6. Father (3)

1 S	2 C	A	3 R	F
■	O	■	O	■
4 R	O	5 U	N	6 D
I	■	S	■	A
7 B		A		D

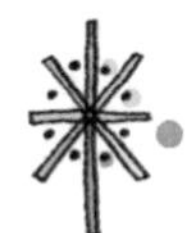

After each clue you can see how many letters the answer has, and whether it contains one word or more.

If you get stuck, or your words don't seem to fit, you can check all the answers at the back of the book.

Happy Christmas puzzling!

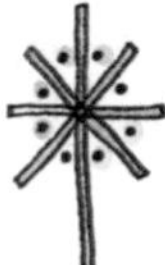

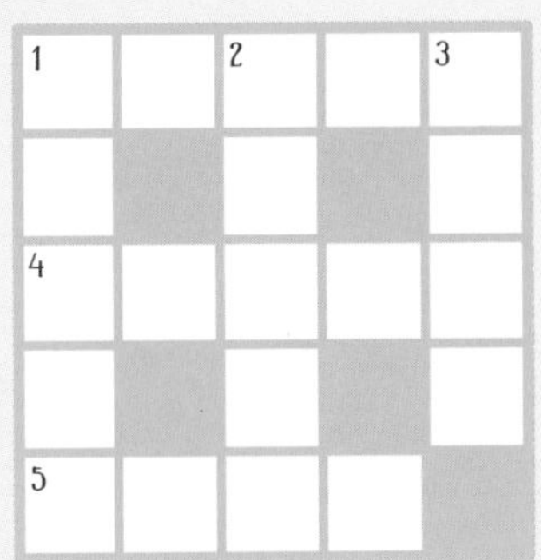

ACROSS

1. We wish you a _____ Christmas (5)
4. The noise an angry dog makes (5)
5. List of actors in a show (4)

DOWN

1. The power to do impossible things (5)
2. These hold a plant in the ground (5)
3. The yellow of an egg (4)

2

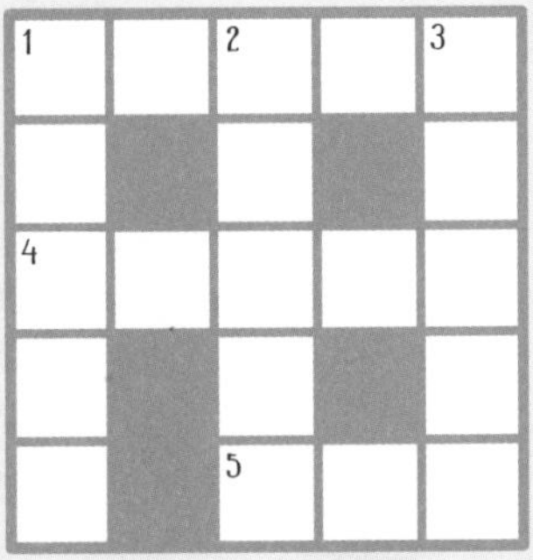

1		2		3
	■		■	
4				
	■		■	
	■	5		

ACROSS

1. Jingle _____! (5)
4. Way, course (5)
5. Jump on one leg (3)

DOWN

1. Christmas celebrates the _____ of Jesus (5)
2. Chuckle (5)
3. Snooze, slumber (5)

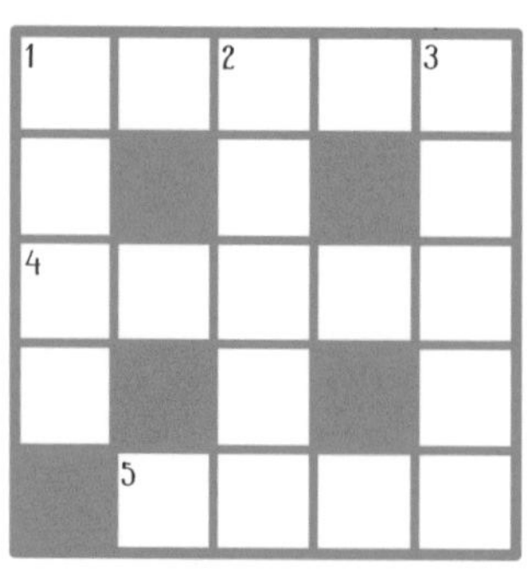

ACROSS

1. Rail-riding vehicle (5)
4. Not old (5)
5. Opposite of east (4)

DOWN

1. Fun things to play with (4)
2. Entertain (5)
3. Santa delivers presents during the _____ (5)

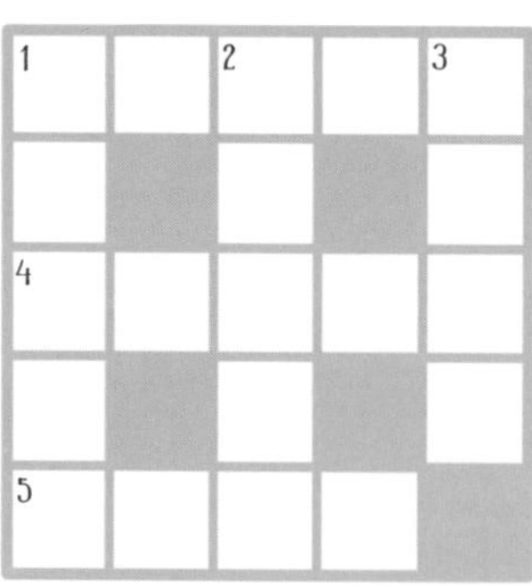

ACROSS

1. Pastime, interest (5)
4. Type of race where runners pass a baton to teammates (5)
5. Simple (4)

DOWN

1. Animal you ride (5)
2. These can be rolled, kicked or thrown (5)
3. Toy that goes up and down on a string (2-2)

ACROSS

1. & 4. Cuddly toys (5, 5)

5. Ache, long, pine (5)

DOWN

1. Cat with a patterned coat (5)
2. Serious play (5)
3. Opposite of no (3)

6

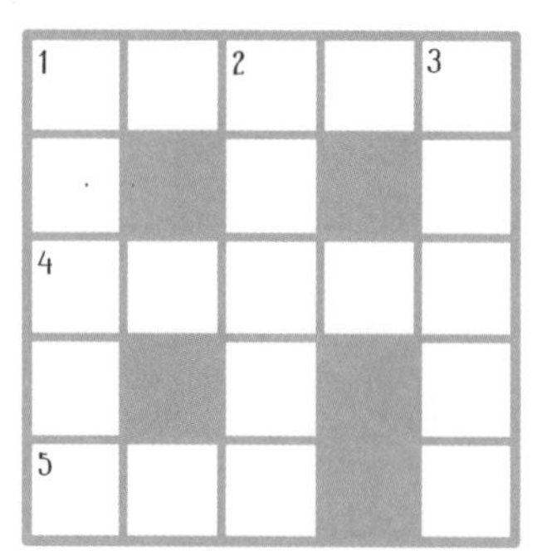

ACROSS

1. Dog noises (5)
4. Poisonous snake (5)
5. Use a chair (3)

DOWN

1. Slang for dollars (5)
2. Machine that can perform complex tasks by itself (5)
3. Pointed, knifelike (5)

7

ACROSS

2. You wear these to keep warm outside (5)
4. Foot-joint (5)

DOWN

1. Fish are often kept in these (5)
2. Tight-lipped shellfish (4)
3. Hot dish of meat or vegetables slowly cooked in gravy (4)

ACROSS

1. Slang for cold (5)
4. In the song, how many maids a-milking did my true love send to me? (5)
5. Place for fitness training (3)

DOWN

1. Another name for Christmas (4)
2. "This little _____ went to market…" (5)
3. Legendary apeman of the Himalayas (4)

9

ACROSS

1. Perhaps (5)
4. Domed house made of ice (5)
5. Wild animal (5)

DOWN

2. The shape made where two straight lines meet at a point (5)
3. Tough footwear (5)

10

ACROSS

1. Lamp (5)
4. Places with many paths, where you can easily get lost (5)
5. Opposite of even (3)

DOWN

1. Young sheep (4)
2. Stared into the distance (5)
3. Job, duty (4)

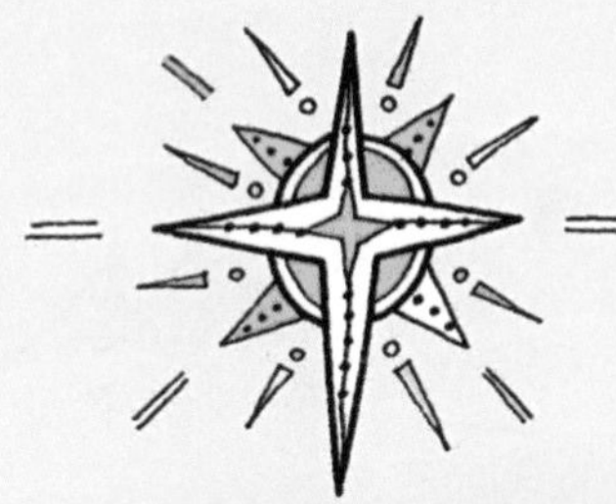

11

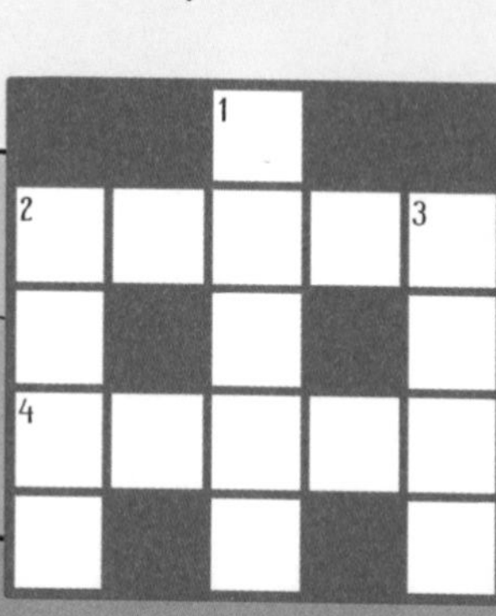

ACROSS

2. Small mountains (5)
4. Fortunate (5)

DOWN

1. Herd of sheep (5)
2. Shining ring around an angel's head (4)
3. Speaks out loud (4)

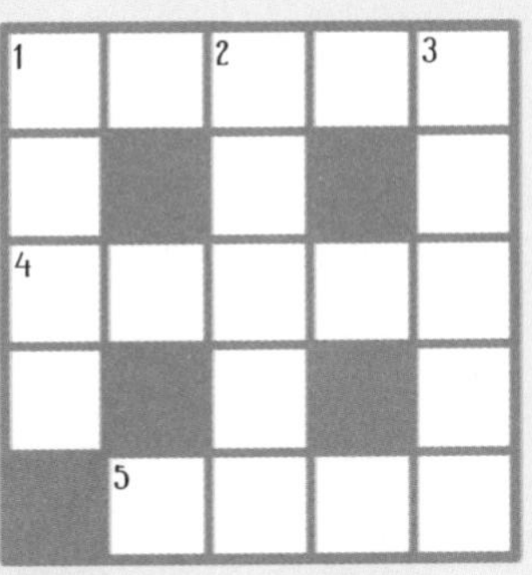

ACROSS

1. (With 3 down) "The angels appeared to the shepherds, singing '_____ on _____, goodwill to men'" (5, 5)
4. Group of church singers (5)
5. Slang for "yes" (4)

DOWN

1. Choose (4)
2. In a higher position (5)
3. (See 1 across)

13

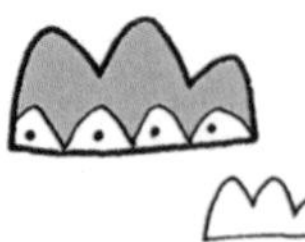

ACROSS

2. "On the fourth day of Christmas, my true love sent to me four calling _____" (5)
4. Presented as a gift (5)

DOWN

1. Meaty sauce (5)
2. Sacks, holdalls (4)
3. Make music with your voice (4)

14

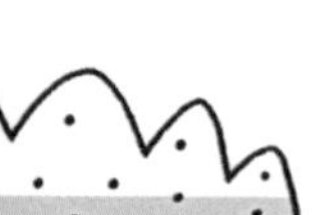

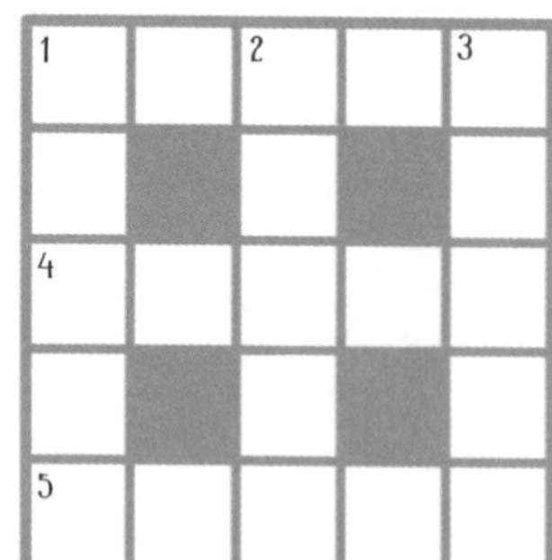

ACROSS

1. Farm bird (5)
4. Occasion (5)
5. Nice to eat (5)

DOWN

1. Visitor at your house (5)
2. Stoves (5)
3. Door (5)

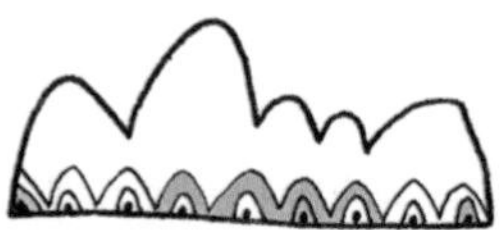

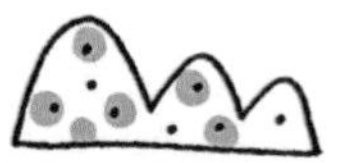

1		2		3
4				
	5			

ACROSS

1. In the song, my true love sent to me seven _____ a-swimming (5)
4. In the song, how many French hens did my true love send to me? (5)
5. In the song, what kind of tree was the partridge in? (4)

DOWN

1. Spot, location (4)
2. Share the same opinion (5)
3. Guide a vehicle (5)

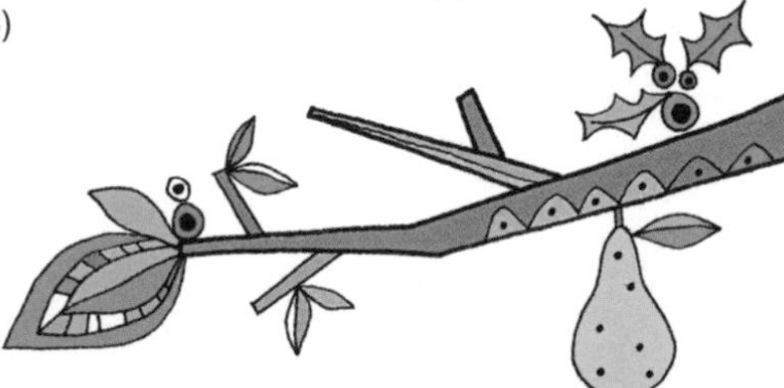

16

1		2		
3				4
	5			

ACROSS

1. In the Christmas song, Santa Claus is coming to where? (4)
3. Very loud (5)
5. List of meal choices (4)

DOWN

1. In the song, how many lords a-leaping did my true love send to me? (3)
2. What kind of Christmas was Bing Crosby dreaming of in the best-selling single of all time? (5)
4. In her festive hit, what is all that Mariah Carey wants for Christmas? (3)

17

ACROSS

4. "'Twas the night before Christmas, and all through the _____" (5)
5. Foot-operated control (5)

DOWN

1. "I saw three _____ come sailing in on Christmas Day in the morning" (5)
2. ____ *Lang Syne*, New Year's song (4)
3. Stomach (5)

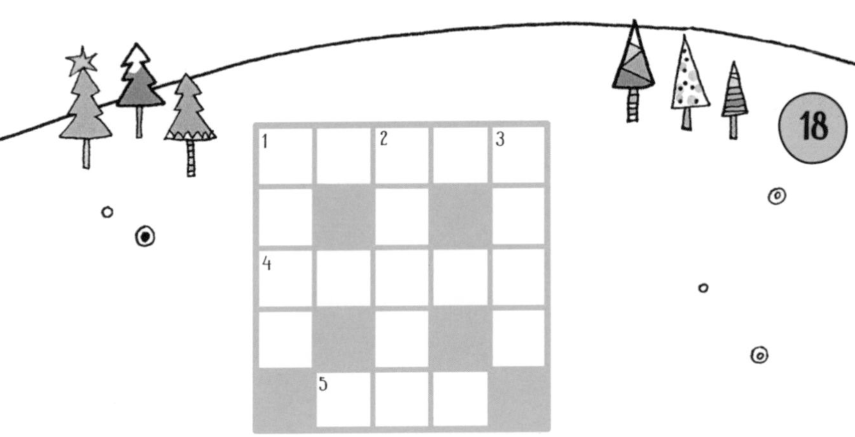

18

ACROSS

1. Yell, holler (5)
4. Small unit of weight (5)
5. Cook in oil (3)

DOWN

1. *Let it ____! Let it ____! Let it ____!* Christmas song written in 1945 (4)
2. One who possesses a thing (5)
3. *Rockin' Around the Christmas* ____, song by Brenda Lee (4)

19

1		2		3
4				
5				

ACROSS

1. An oak tree grows from this (5)
4. It comes in shades such as emerald, olive and lime (5)
5. If someone gives up a bad habit, they are said to have turned over a new ____ (4)

DOWN

1. Winged heavenly messenger sometimes seen perching on top of Christmas trees (5)
2. High-class musical, often sung in Italian (5)
3. In the song, how many ladies dancing did my true love send to me? (4)

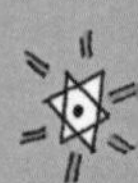

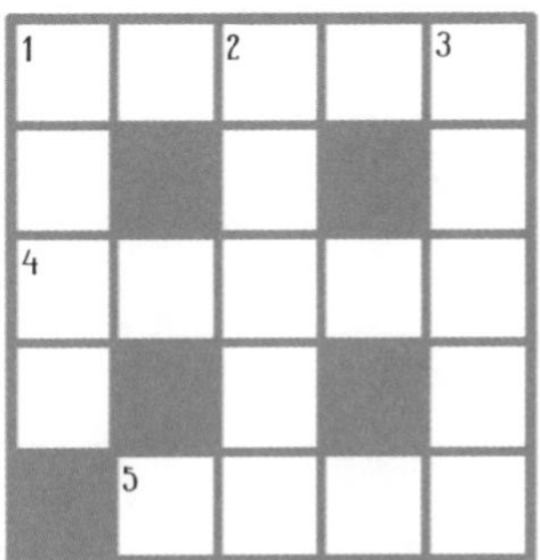

20

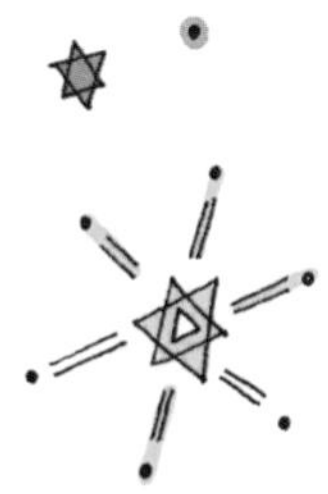

ACROSS

1. "When the _____ breaks, the cradle will fall..." (5)
4. Give off light (5)
5. You see with these (4)

DOWN

1. Active, on the go (4)
2. Togetherness (5)
3. The backs of your feet (5)

21

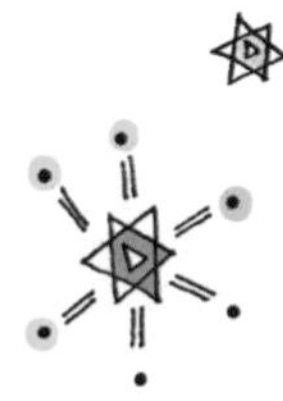

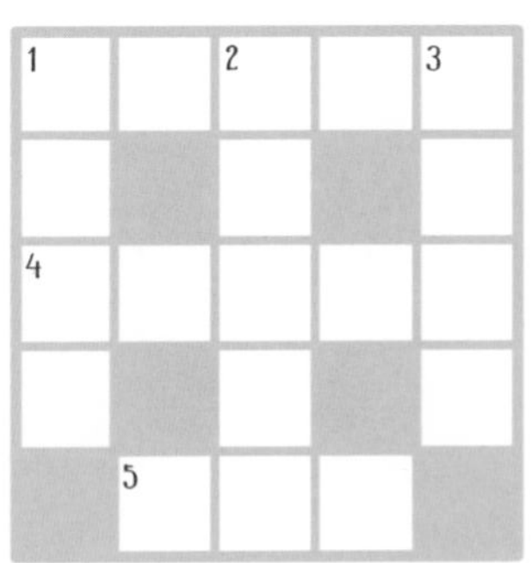

ACROSS

1. Presents (5)
4. Small fruit, green, purple or black, often pickled in salt water (5)
5. Dr. ___ travels through time and space in a blue police box (3)

DOWN

1. Gently shine (4)
2. Belief, trust (5)
3. Appear to be (4)

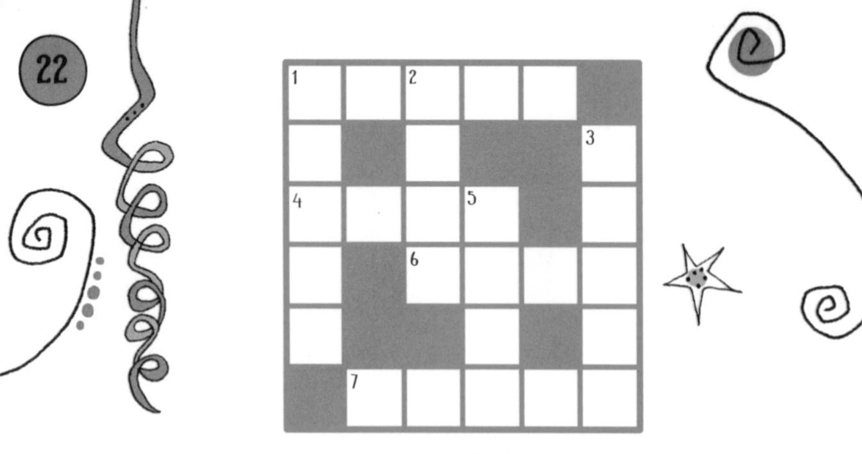

ACROSS

1. These are often used to send Christmas greetings (5)
4. On top of (4)
6. Untidiness (4)
7. Conceals (5)

DOWN

1. Hints (5)
2. Living ____ or dining ____ (4)
3. Expenses (5)
5. Require (4)

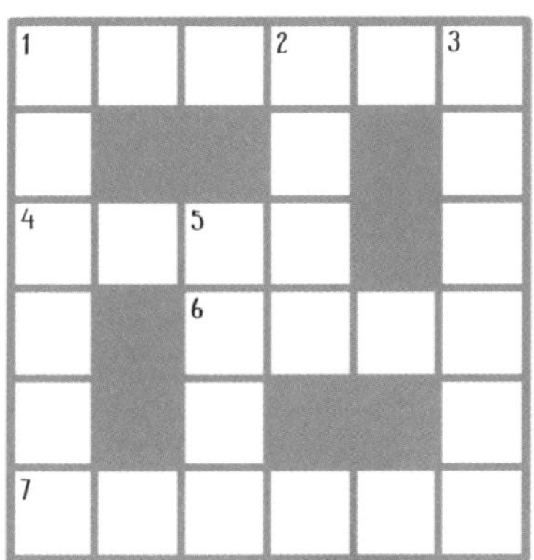

ACROSS

1. Bright strip of material used to decorate gifts (6)
4. Not fast (4)
6. Is not (4)
7. Even so (6)

DOWN

1. The world's largest country (6)
2. Loopy knots made of 1 across (4)
3. Tidily (6)
5. Greasy (4)

24

ACROSS

1. ____ office, where you send packages and mail (4)
5. Said when you discover something (3)
6. Cover a gift in paper (4)
8. Receives (4)
10. View, regard (3)
11. Remain (4)

DOWN

2. You use this to row a boat (3)
3. Roll of sticky, clear plastic (4)
4. Gift labels (4)
6. Hope, desire (4)
7. "It's been ____ since I've seen you!" (4)
9. A hot drink (3)

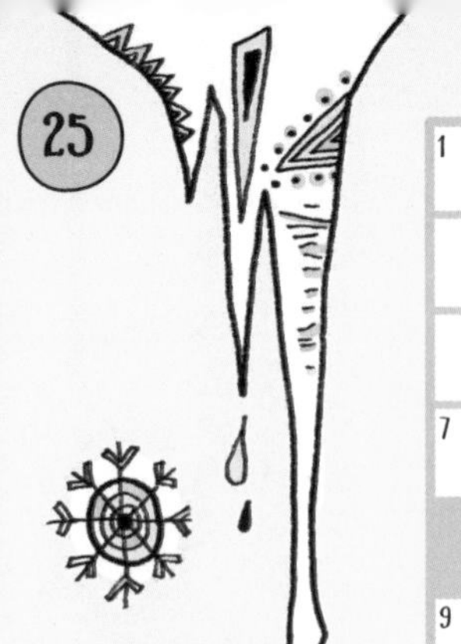

25

1		2		3	
	■		■		■
	■	4	5		6
7	8			■	
■		■		■	
9					

ACROSS

1. The coldest season (6)
4. Mash with your teeth (4)
7. Similar to (4)
9. Humans (6)

DOWN

1. Sweaters are often made of this (4)
2. A scarf goes around this part of you (4)
3. December 24th is Christmas ___ (3)
5. Pile (4)
6. Move your hand to say hello or goodbye (4)
8. Frozen water (3)

26

1			2	■	3
	■	■	4		
5		6		■	
	■	7			
8			■	■	
	■	9			

ACROSS

1. Blaze, inferno (4)
4. Fib (3)
5. Cereal grains used to make a warming breakfast (4)
7. Stop (4)
8. Long period, age (3)
9. Dress in (4)

DOWN

1. Disney movie about a princess with magical power over ice and snow (6)
2. The name of the princess in 1 down (4)
3. Electric warming device (6)
6. Defrost (4)

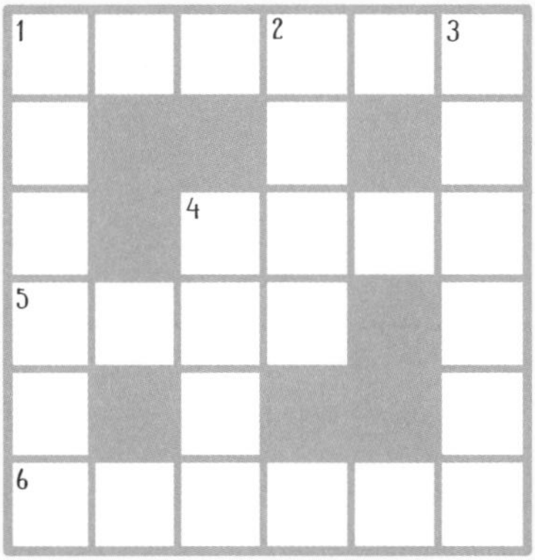

1			2		3
		4			
5					
6					

ACROSS

1. Frozen drip (6)
4. What the wind does (4)
5. Grew older (4)
6. Lengthen (6)

DOWN

1. Chilly cartoon movie series about the adventures of some prehistoric animals (3, 3)
2. Opposite of hot (4)
3. In the movie ______ *Scissorhands*, the title character uses his blade-like fingers to carve an ice sculpture (6)
4. Opposite of worst (4)

28

1		2			3
	■		■	■	
	■	4	5		
6				■	
	■	■		■	
7					

ACROSS

1. The Three Kings who visited Jesus are often pictured riding these (6)
4. What the Three Kings followed to find Jesus (4)
6. The Three Kings are also known as the Three ____ Men (4)
7. Open-toed shoe (6)

DOWN

1. Kings' or queens' special hats often made of precious metal and jewels (6)
2. Fail to hit a target (4)
3. Move up or down a screen (6)
5. Look after, care for (4)

29

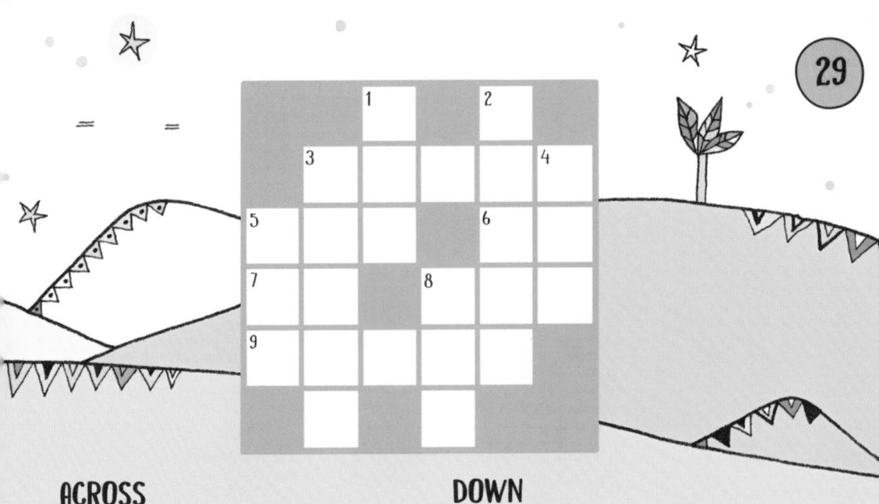

ACROSS

3. One of the Three Kings' gifts, a type of fragrant resin (5)
5. Enemy (3)
6. In the morning (1.1.)
7. @ (2)
8. Belonging to him (3)
9. Regal (5)

DOWN

1. This is used to stain clothes, or hair (3)
2. Path, track (5)
3. Engine (5)
4. This often goes in front of the name of British Royal Navy ships (1.1.1.)
5. Distant (3)
8. Did have (3)

30

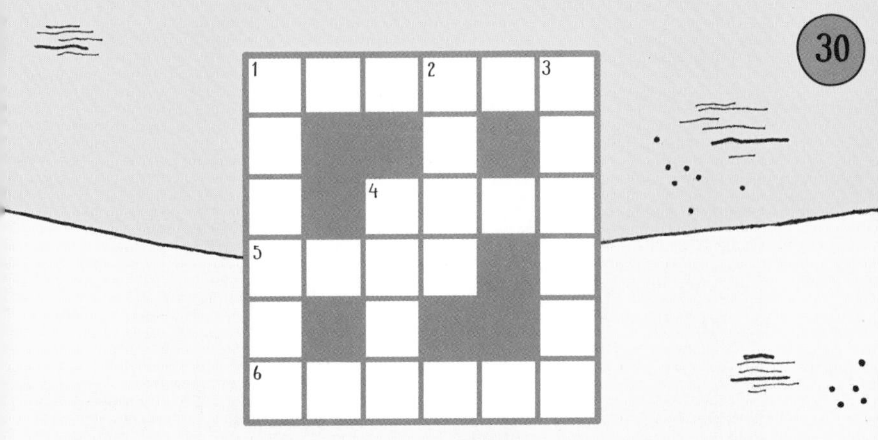

ACROSS

1. Shining or clever (6)
4. Opposite of west (4)
5. One of the Three Kings' gifts (4)
6. Charms, magic words (6)

DOWN

1. Scouts and sheriffs both wear these (6)
2. Happy, relieved (4)
3. Names of books or movies (6)
4. French for "she"; girl's name (4)

1			2		3
	■	■		■	
	■	4			
5				■	
	■		■	■	
■	6				

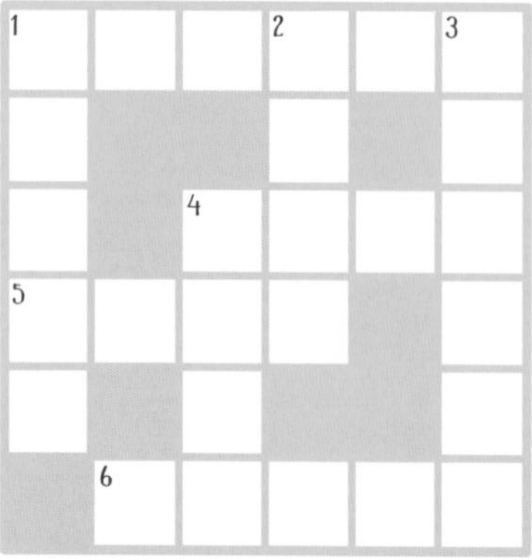

ACROSS

1. In Charles Dickens's *A Christmas Carol*, Ebenezer Scrooge's miserable catchphrase was "Bah! ______!" (6)
4. Salvador ____, Spanish painter famed for his bizarre art (4)
5. Opposite of shut (4)
6. Half-melted snow (5)

DOWN

1. King of Israel who tried to kill the baby Jesus (5)
2. Haricot or runner, for example (4)
3. In a book by Dr. Seuss, a mean, green, furry creature who tries to steal Christmas (6)
4. Hand out the cards before a game (4)

32

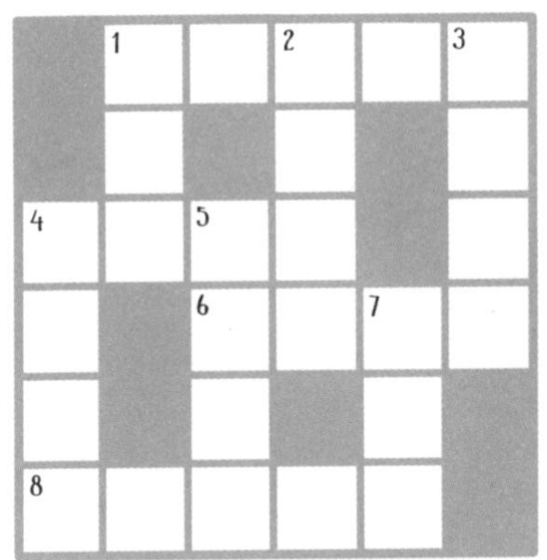

ACROSS

1. Cruella __ ___, the fur-loving villainess of *101 Dalmatians* (2, 3)
4. Loathsome, disgusting (4)
6. What the Sun does at dusk (4)
8. Horrible, spiteful (5)

DOWN

1. Double-act (3)
2. Unpleasant, wicked (4)
3. Falsehoods (4)
4. Native of Finland (4)
5. Employs (4)
7. Attempt (3)

33

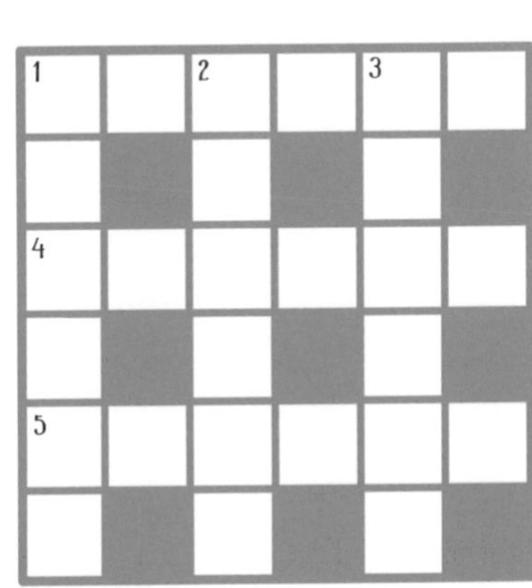

ACROSS

1. Oogie ______, sack-cloth villain of *The Nightmare Before Christmas* (6)
4. Smelly vegetables that can make you cry (6)
5. Breaks rules in order to win (6)

DOWN

1. Decorative breast-pin (6)
2. ______ Twist, orphan boy in a book by Dickens (6)
3. Light, set on fire (6)

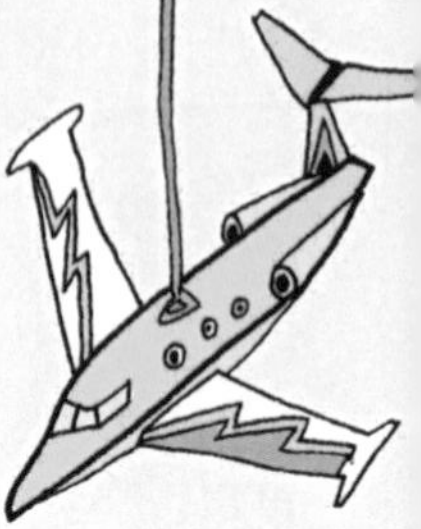

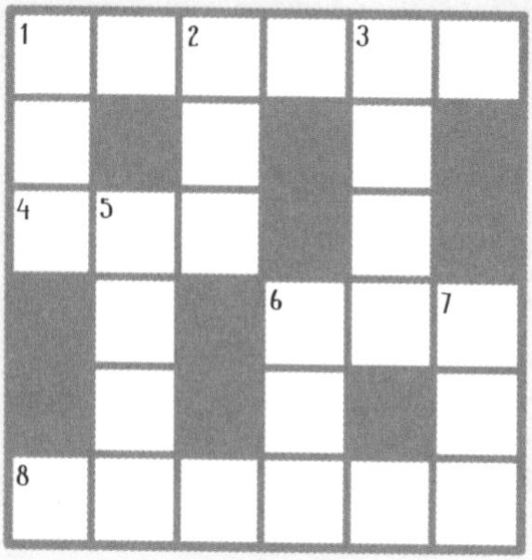

34

1		2		3	
4	5				
			6		7
8					

ACROSS

1. Winged vehicles (6)
4. Request (3)
6. Supersonic aircraft (3)
8. Protective headgear (6)

DOWN

1. *The Princess and the* ___, fairy tale (3)
2. The boat Noah built (3)
3. One of North America's Great Lakes (4)
5. Certain (4)
6. Fruit preserve (3)
7. Make a disapproving noise (3)

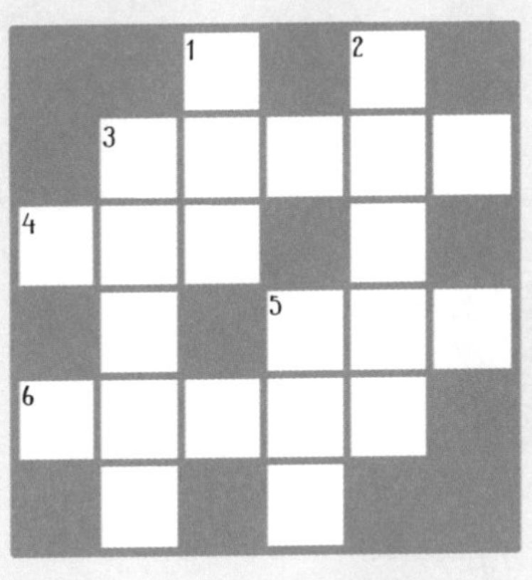

ACROSS

3. Two-wheeled vehicles (5)
4. Someone's male child (3)
5. Weep (3)
6. Homeless cat or dog (5)

DOWN

1. Be victorious (3)
2. Vessel used to cross a river or a short distance at sea (5)
3. Small ships (5)
5. Automobile (3)

36

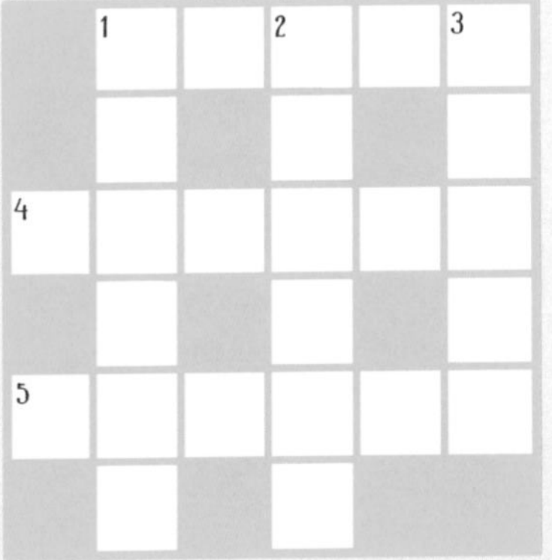

ACROSS

1. This word describes clothes that are roomy or oversized (5)
4. Big ship used to carry fuel (6)
5. Black and white horse-like animals from Africa (6)

DOWN

1. Controls for slowing or stopping a vehicle (6)
2. Small vehicle used in racing for fun (2, 4)
3. Units of measurement equal to 3 feet (5)

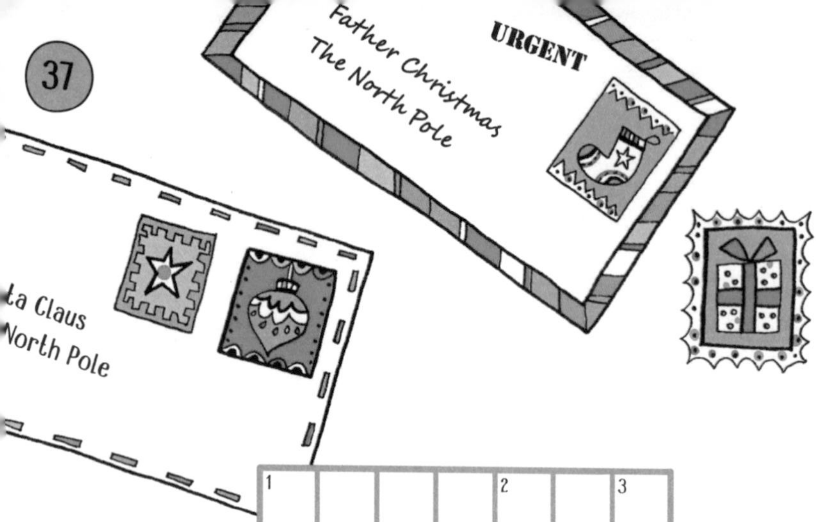

Father Christmas
The North Pole
URGENT

ta Claus
North Pole

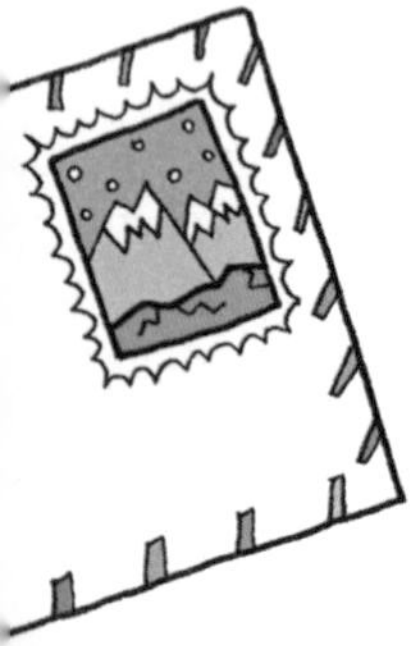

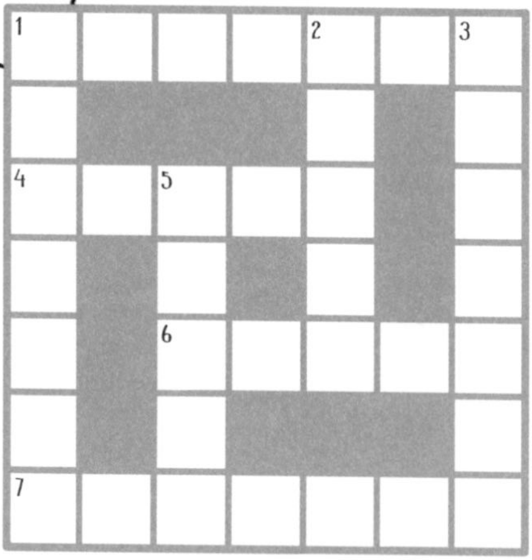

1				2		3
	■	■	■		■	
4		5			■	
	■		■		■	
	■	6				
	■		■	■	■	
7						

ACROSS

1. Santa receives millions of these every year (7)
4. Very angry (5)
6. Part of a flower (5)
7. Graceful, dignified (7)

DOWN

1. Spare time, relaxation (7)
2. Choose someone by voting (5)
3. Bright red (7)
5. Crunchy fruit (5)

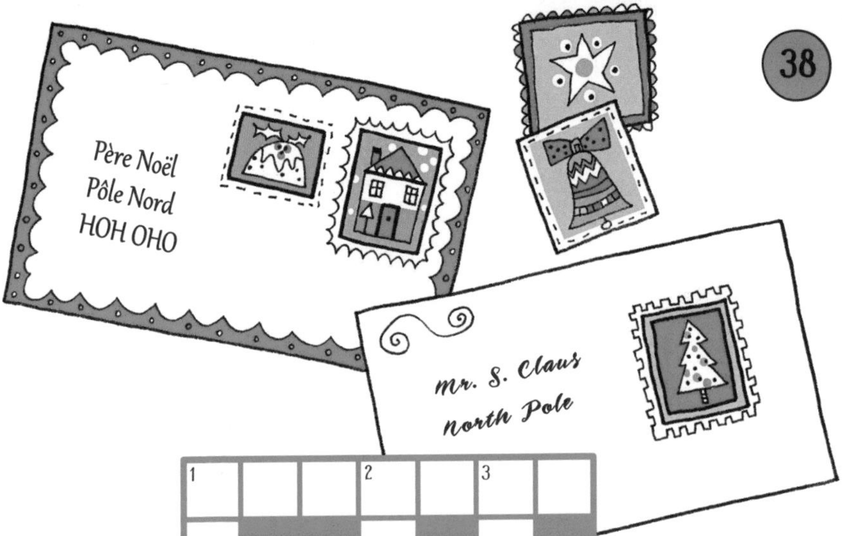

38

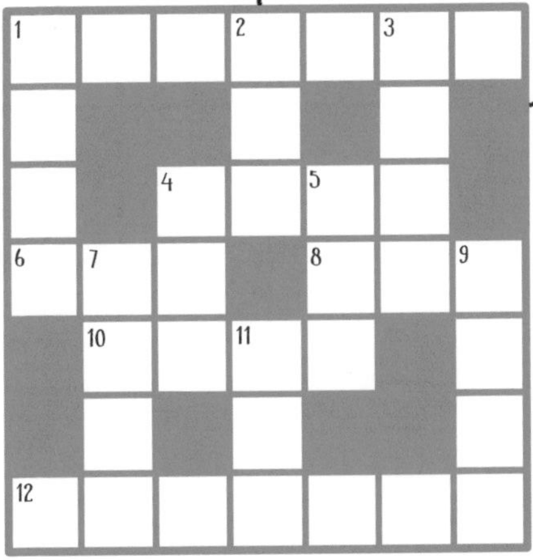

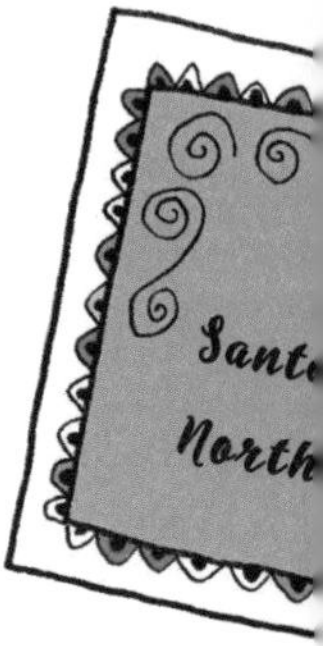

Père Noël
Pôle Nord
HOH OHO

Mr. S. Claus
North Pole

1			2		3	
		4		5		
6	7			8		9
	10		11			
12						

ACROSS

1. (with 1 down) "He's making a list, he's checking it twice, he's gonna find out who's _______ or ____" (7, 4)
4. What people used to say 1 across children would find in their stockings (4)
6. Ostrich-like Australian bird (3)
8. Santa's outfit is ___ and white (3)
10. Individual thing, especially in a list (4)
12. Mixed with a spoon (7)

DOWN

1. (See 1 across)
2. Slime (3)
3. Story (4)
4. Snip (3)
5. Upper limb (3)
7. Light fog (4)
9. Action, achievement (4)
11. Organ of hearing (3)

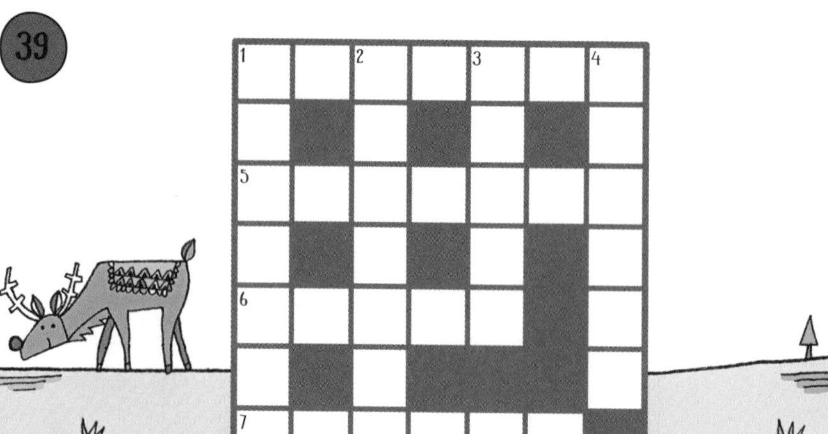

ACROSS

1. This one of Santa's reindeer might be good at leaping around (7)
5. Effort, try (7)
6. Snoozed (5)
7. This one of Santa's reindeer sounds very fast (6)

DOWN

1. Complimented, applauded (7)
2. These grow on reindeer's heads (7)
3. This one of Santa's reindeer shares its name with a light that travels slowly through the night sky (5)
4. Baby's noisy toy (6)

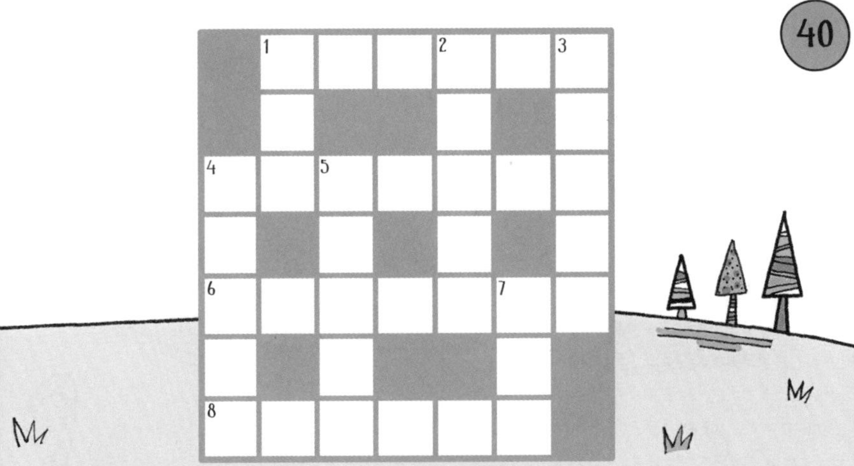

ACROSS

1. Of all Santa's reindeer, this one sounds like it has the best sense of rhythm (6)
4. What nationality is Tintin? (7)
6. The red-nosed reindeer (7)
8. ______ Schwarzenegger, Austrian-American movie star (6)

DOWN

1. A female deer (3)
2. Cool something down (5)
3. Large cattle farm (5)
4. South East Asian country also known as Myanmar (5)
5. Burdened, loaded up (5)
7. Peas grow in one of these (3)

41

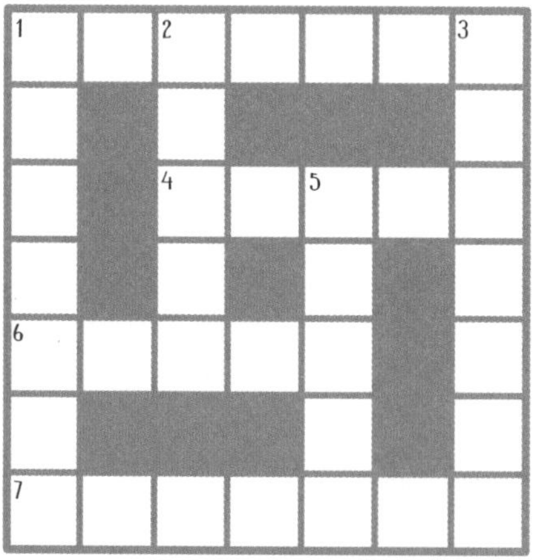

1		2				3
		4		5		
6						
7						

ACROSS

1. Nuts often used in baking, whole, flaked or ground (7)
4. Principled, virtuous (5)
6. Opposite of closes (5)
7. Christmas chocolate roll cake (4, 3)

DOWN

1. "Hello! Is _______ home?" (7)
2. _____ pies, traditional British Christmas treats, which sound as though they contain meat (5)
3. Looking for (7)
5. Leafy, green herb used to make pesto (5)

42

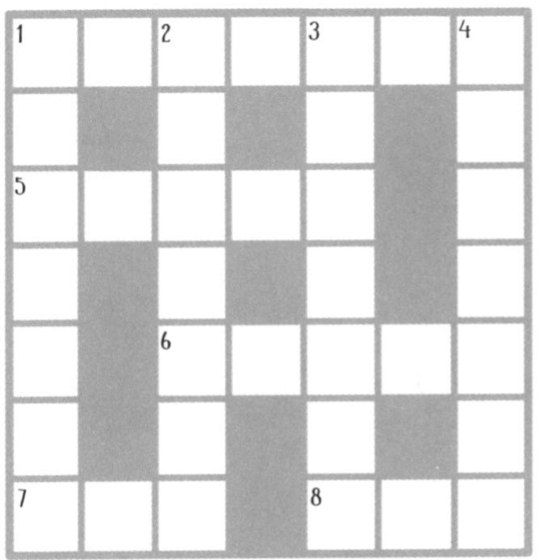

ACROSS

1. Chocolate chip _______, sweet baked goods (7)
5. Walnut-like nut used in cakes and sweet pies (5)
6. You wear this when baking (5)
7. Finish (3)
8. Distress signal (1.1.1.)

DOWN

1. Small cake for one person (7)
2. Garden of fruit trees (7)
3. Refuses to notice (7)
4. Another helping (7)

43

ACROSS

1. Married woman (4)
5. Person built out of snow (7)
6. *Baby, It's Cold* _______, Christmas duet sung by a man and woman (7)
7. Inquires (4)

DOWN

1. Good judgement (6)
2. A 5 across who appears in a famous Christmas song (6)
3. Electronic letters (6)
4. Snow ______, shapes made by lying down in the snow and moving your arms and legs (6)

		1			2	
3						
4	5			6		7
8						

ACROSS

3. Tools for digging, or clearing snow (7)
4. Season when there is no school or work (7)
8. Orange vegetables often used for snowmen's noses (7)

DOWN

1. Pleasantly cold; calm under pressure (4)
2. Jumping, biting insect (4)
3. Be quiet! (3)
5. Friendly snowman in the movie *Frozen* (4)
6. Entrance (4)
7. Positive answer (3)

45

ACROSS

2. This fits into a lock (3)
5. Knot-shaped German bread (7)
6. German fruit bread eaten at Christmas (7)

DOWN

1. *Harry Potter and the _______ Hallows* (7)
3. The opposite of a lie (5)
4. Not as many (5)

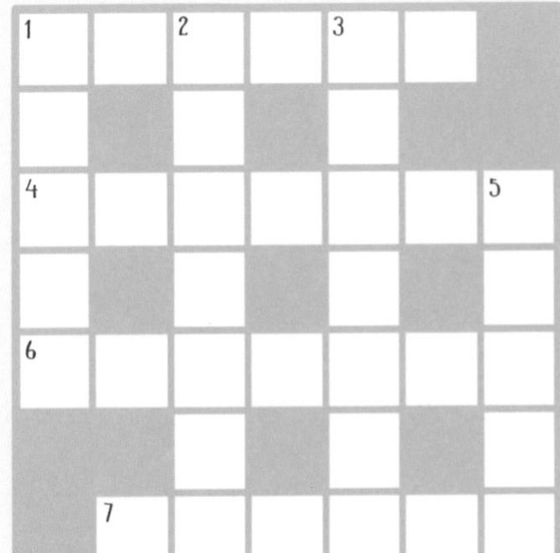

ACROSS

1. Queen Victoria's German husband, who helped to popularize Christmas trees in England (6)
4. The sounds in people's voices that tell you where they come from (7)
6. A Frankfurter, for example (7)
7. Capital of Germany (6)

DOWN

1. Amy _____, US actress who starred in *Enchanted* (5)
2. "He was sad _______ his fish died." (7)
3. _______ Boggs – sneaky purple lizard who's Sulley's rival in *Monsters Inc.* (7)
5. Serious, strict (5)

1	2			3	■	4
■		■	■		■	
5		6				
	■		■		■	
7					8	
	■		■	■		■
	■	9				

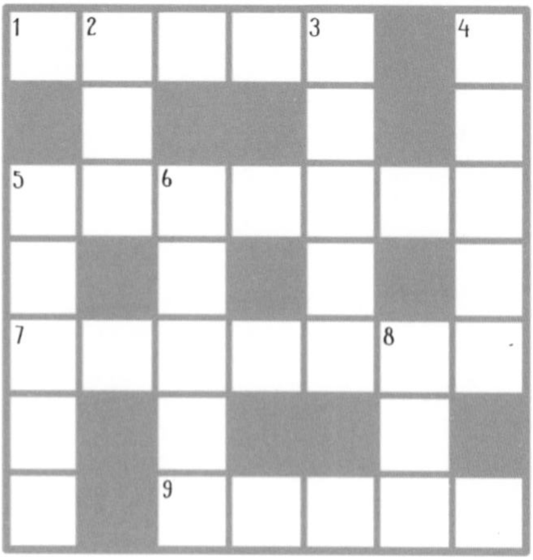

ACROSS

1. Traditional Christmas song (5)
5. Great ________, the large island containing England, Scotland and Wales (7)
7. Eternal (7)
9. On your own (5)

DOWN

2. *Walking in the ___*, song from the animated movie *The Snowman* (3)
3. Depart (5)
4. Christmas song: *We Three _____ of Orient Are* (5)
5. Christmas song: *In the _____ Midwinter* (5)
6. Large South Asian country (5)
8. It rises daily (3)

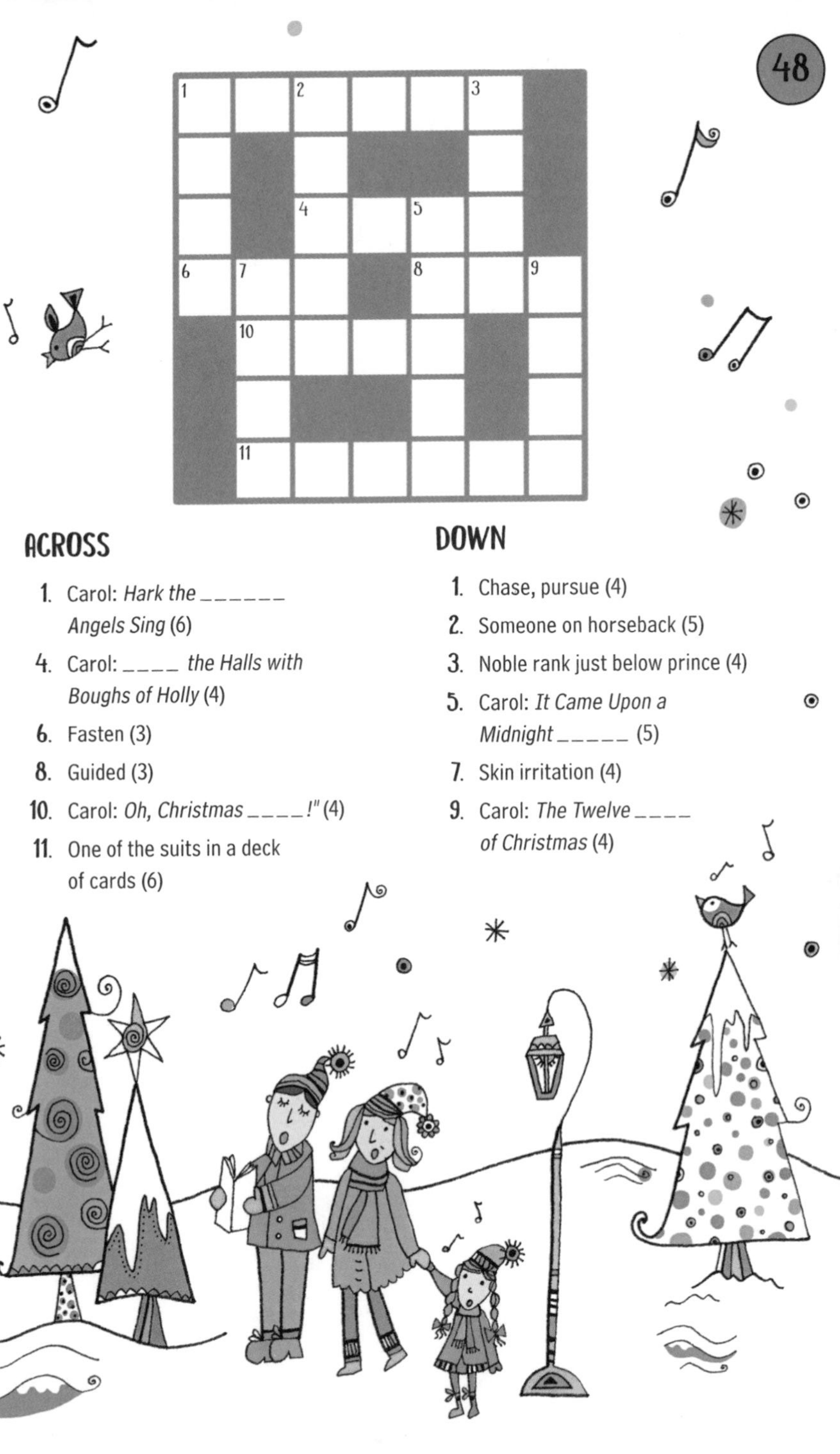

ACROSS

1. Carol: *Hark the ______ Angels Sing* (6)
4. Carol: ____ *the Halls with Boughs of Holly* (4)
6. Fasten (3)
8. Guided (3)
10. Carol: *Oh, Christmas ____!"* (4)
11. One of the suits in a deck of cards (6)

DOWN

1. Chase, pursue (4)
2. Someone on horseback (5)
3. Noble rank just below prince (4)
5. Carol: *It Came Upon a Midnight _____* (5)
7. Skin irritation (4)
9. Carol: *The Twelve ____ of Christmas* (4)

49

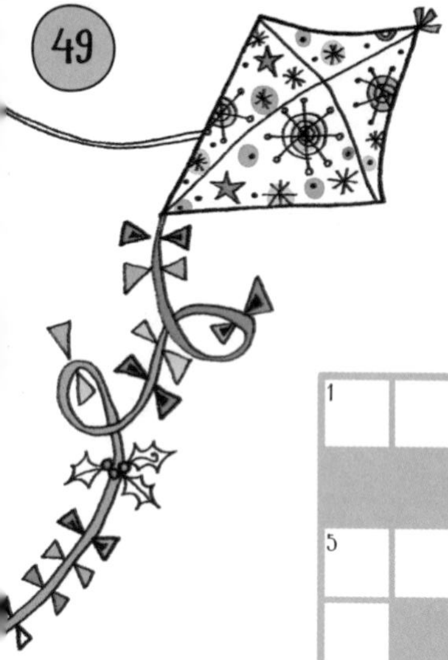

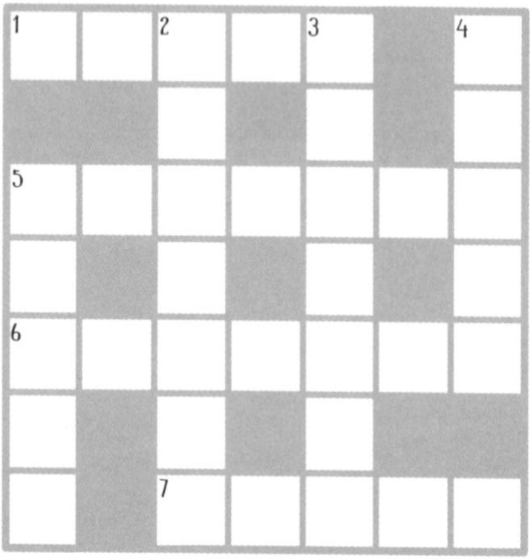

1		2		3	■	4
■	■		■		■	
5						
	■		■		■	
6						
	■		■		■	■
	■	7				

ACROSS

1. Toys that fly on a string (5)
5. _______ *Pursuit*, quiz boardgame (7)
6. _______ Prime, leader of the Autobots (7)
7. Less common (5)

DOWN

2. Energetic party game with a spotted mat and a spinner (7)
3. Michael Phelps, for example (7)
4. Toy people you dress up (5)
5. The _____ Fairy may leave you money in return for something that fell out (5)

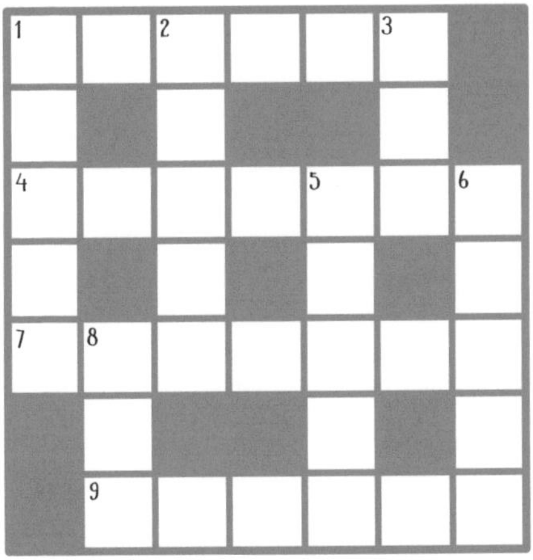

50

1		2			3	■
	■		■	■		■
4				5		6
	■		■		■	
7	8					
■		■	■		■	
■	9					

ACROSS

1. World-famous doll with a boyfriend named Ken (6)
4. Talked gibberish (7)
7. Natives of Alaska and Siberia famous for their fur-lined coats (7)
9. Springy toy that can walk down stairs (6)

DOWN

1. Holy book (5)
2. Erno _____, Hungarian inventor of a puzzling cube (5)
3. Hole in a needle (3)
5. Sour, yellow fruit (5)
6. Unswept (5)
8. Short for sister (3)

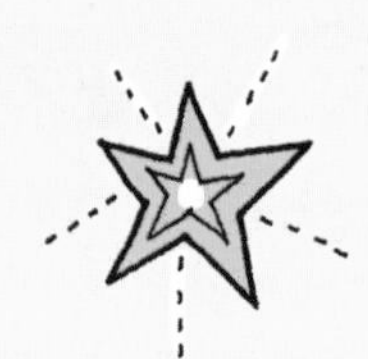

1		2		3		4
5			6			
7		8		9		
10						

ACROSS

1. "Now bring us some figgy _______" from the carol, *We Wish You a Merry Christmas* (7)
5. (with 6 down) This American dessert, eaten at Christmas and Thanksgiving, might also make you think of Halloween (7, 3)
7. Extreme, passionate (7)
10. Good mental health (6)

DOWN

1. Young dogs (7)
2. Poorly lit (3)
3. Writing liquid (3)
4. ______bread houses are often built at Christmas time (6)
6. (see 5 across)
8. Can (3)
9. An almond, for example (3)

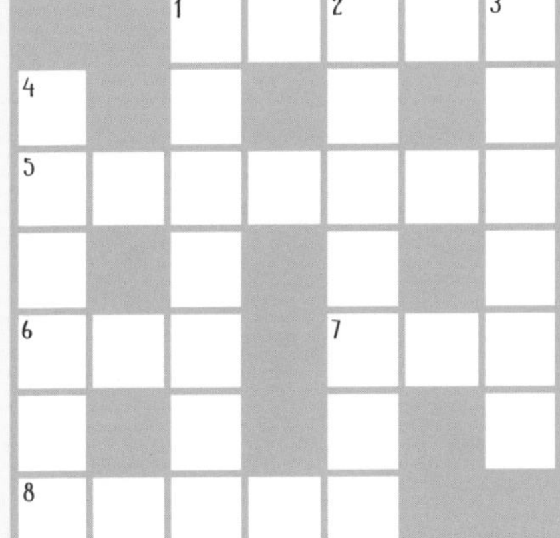

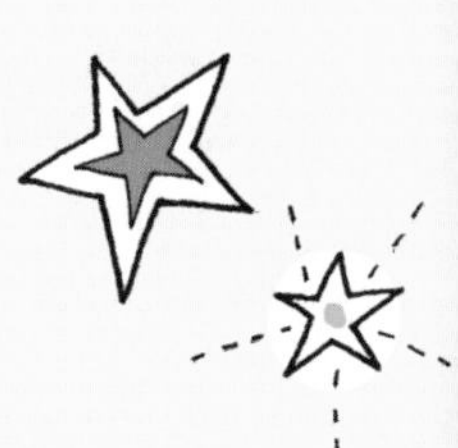

ACROSS

1. The _____ Forest in Germany is famous for its chocolate, cream and cherry dessert cake (5)
5. Tight, one-piece garment worn by dancers and gymnasts (7)
6. Evil deed (3)
7. How old you are (3)
8. Regions (5)

DOWN

1. Small, gooey chocolate cake (7)
2. Characters or icons that stand in for you online or in computer games (7)
3. Bean-shaped organ of the body (6)
4. Baked ______, meringue and ice cream dessert named after the most northerly US state (6)

53

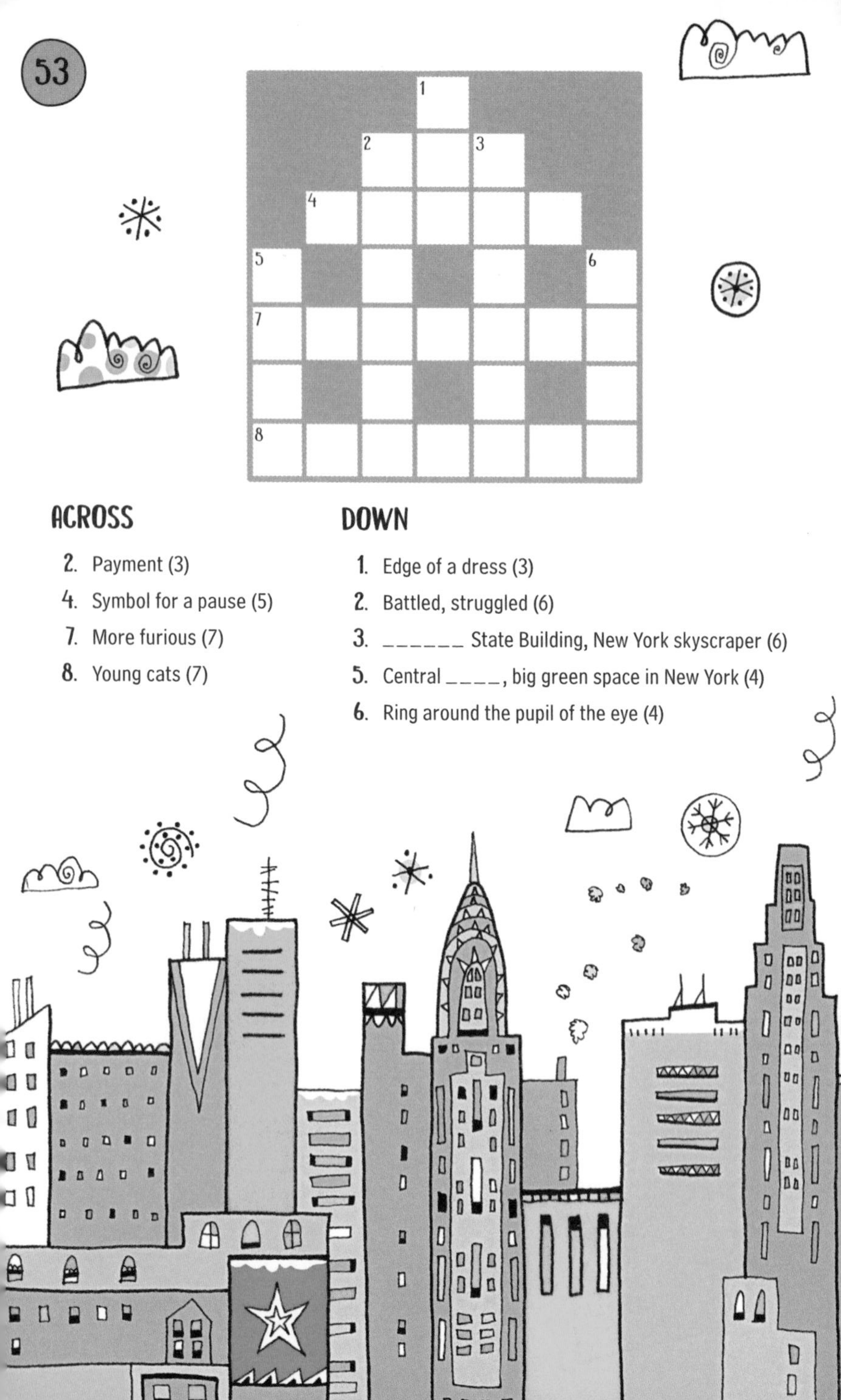

ACROSS

2. Payment (3)
4. Symbol for a pause (5)
7. More furious (7)
8. Young cats (7)

DOWN

1. Edge of a dress (3)
2. Battled, struggled (6)
3. ______ State Building, New York skyscraper (6)
5. Central ____, big green space in New York (4)
6. Ring around the pupil of the eye (4)

54

ACROSS

1. New York is nicknamed the ___ Apple (3)
3. Animal's furry, clawed hand (3)
5. _______ *on 34th Street*, movie about a little girl and a lawyer that try to help an old man who says he's Santa (7)
6. French-style hat (5)
8. Move your head up and down (3)

DOWN

1. Knock into something (4)
2. Area planted with grass, flowers and vegetables (6)
3. Crowded, jammed (6)
4. Each one has seven days (4)
7. Paddle a boat (3)

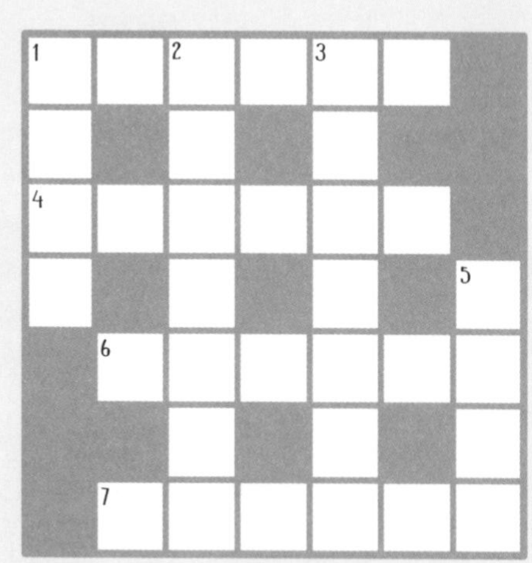

ACROSS

1. (with 1 down) Liquid used to make foam in a tub of water (6, 4)
4. Scented white powder used on skin (6)
6. This keeps a ship from drifting away (6)
7. Field (6)

DOWN

1. (see 1 across)
2. When you manage to keep yours, you don't fall over (7)
3. Giggled (7)
5. Black bird (4)

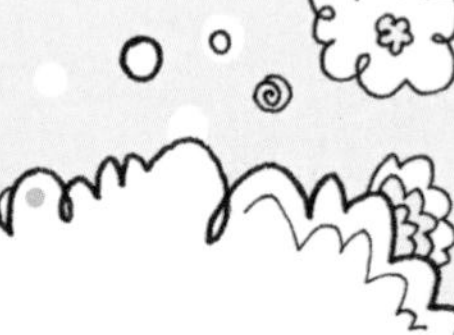

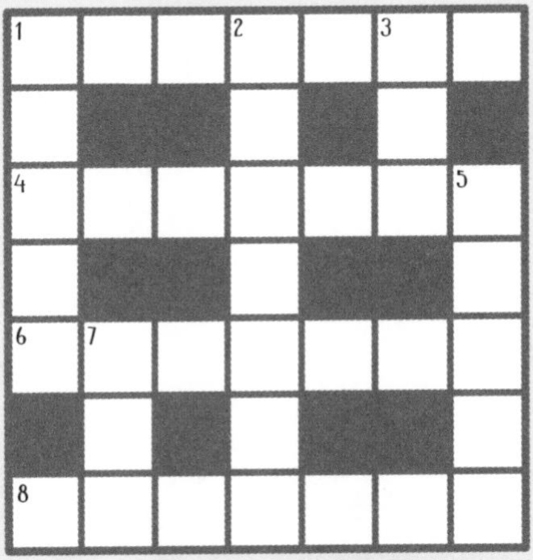

56

1			2		3	
	■	■		■		■
4						5
	■	■		■	■	
6	7					
■		■		■	■	
8						

ACROSS

1. Fragrance, scent (7)
4. Used for cleaning hair (7)
6. Previously (7)
8. Hides, stows away (7)

DOWN

1. Tooth_____, used with a toothbrush (5)
2. Women or girls (7)
3. The noise a cow makes (3)
5. Monsters like Shrek (5)
7. Perform in a play (3)

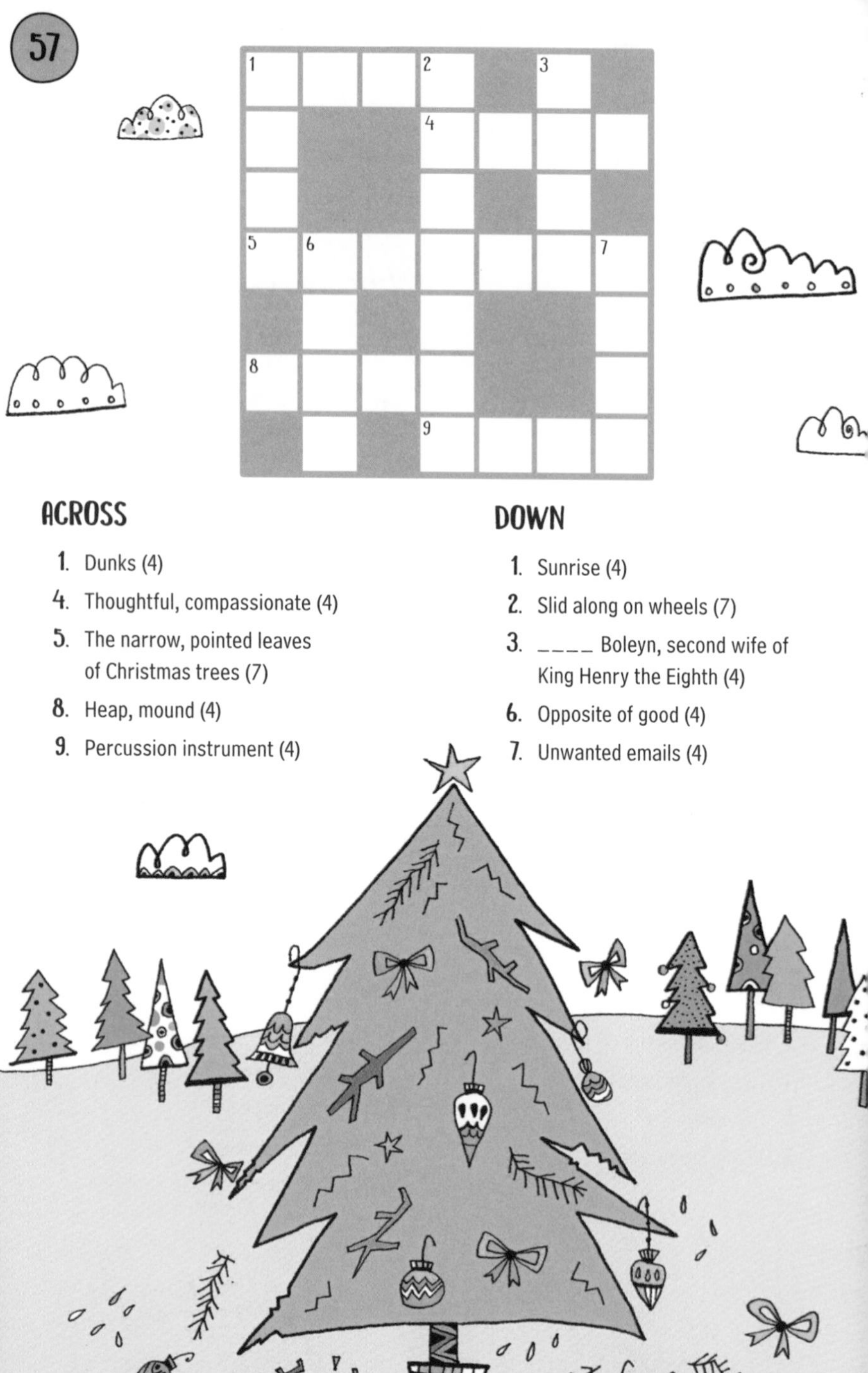

ACROSS

1. Dunks (4)
4. Thoughtful, compassionate (4)
5. The narrow, pointed leaves of Christmas trees (7)
8. Heap, mound (4)
9. Percussion instrument (4)

DOWN

1. Sunrise (4)
2. Slid along on wheels (7)
3. ____ Boleyn, second wife of King Henry the Eighth (4)
6. Opposite of good (4)
7. Unwanted emails (4)

ACROSS

1. Small pool of water (6)
4. Turn to ice (6)
6. The shape of a snail's shell (6)
7. Brand new (6)

DOWN

1. Magic dragon who lived by the sea (4)
2. Pizza style (4-3)
3. Long-tailed reptiles (7)
5. Ran away (4)

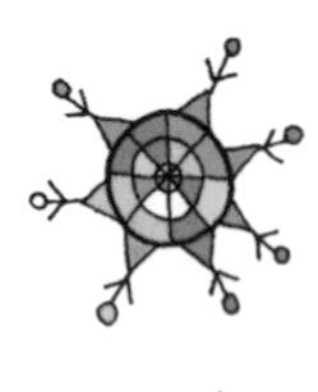

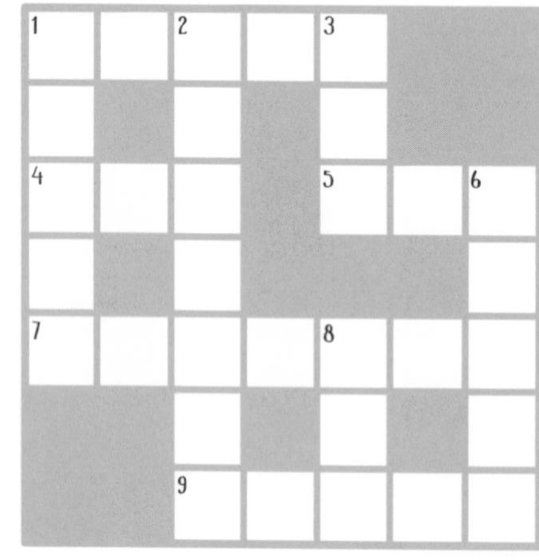

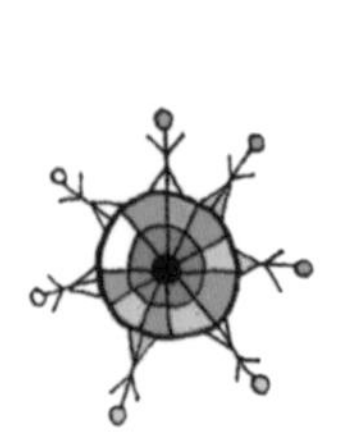

ACROSS

1. Ventriloquist's _____, puppet that sits on a performer's lap and seems to talk by itself (5)
4. Hat with a peak (3)
5. Suggestion (3)
7. Add sugar (7)
9. Slow-moving South American animal that spends most of its life in the trees (5)

DOWN

1. Water birds (5)
2. Kermit and Elmo, for example (7)
3. Up until now (3)
6. Mr. _____, badly-behaved, long-nosed puppet with a wife named Judy (5)
8. As well (3)

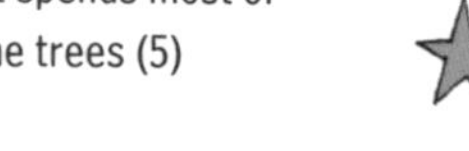

60

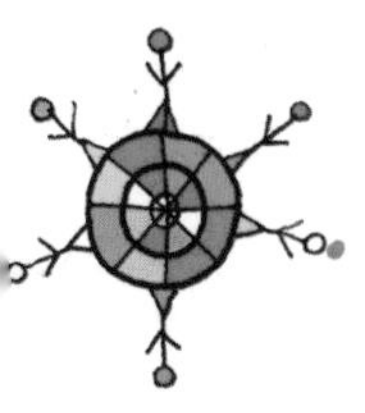

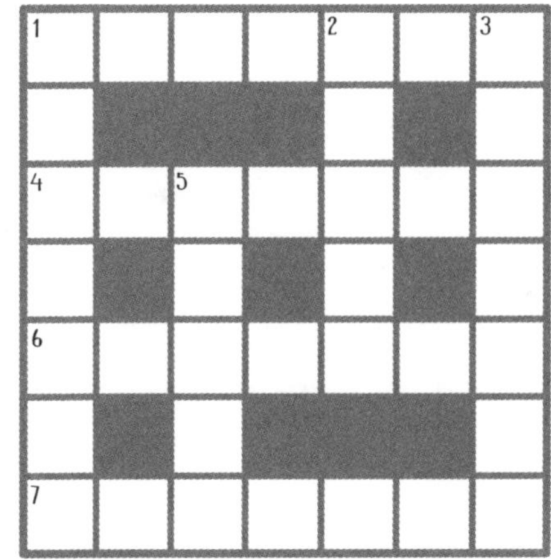

ACROSS

1. Bat and ball sport where players traditionally dress in white (7)
4. Marionettes are puppets with _______ (7)
6. Improved, superior version of a product or service (7)
7. Little jobs, things to do (7)

DOWN

1. Outfit (7)
2. East African country famous for its big wildlife reserves (5)
3. Decorative tufts of thread (7)
5. A pirate flag is known as a Jolly _____ (5)

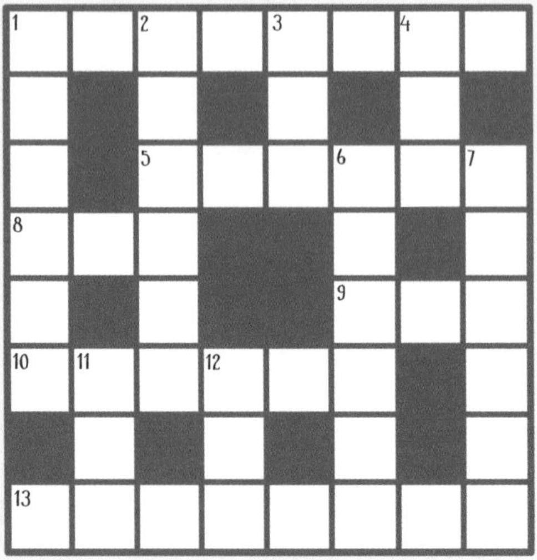

61

1		2		3		4	
	■		■		■		■
	■	5			6		7
8			■	■		■	
	■		■	■	9		
10	11		12			■	
■		■		■		■	
13							

ACROSS

1. Make a room prettier (8)
5. Lords, ladies, aristocrats (6)
8. Help (3)
9. Large area of salt water (3)
10. Britney ______, US pop singer (6)
13. Decorative hangings, sometimes made of leaves or flowers (8)

DOWN

1. Stories you imagine while asleep (6)
2. Wax stick with a wick (6)
3. Steal from someone (3)
4. Draw, equal result (3)
6. Learning session (6)
7. Circles or squares, for example (6)
11. Small, round green vegetable (3)
12. Everything (3)

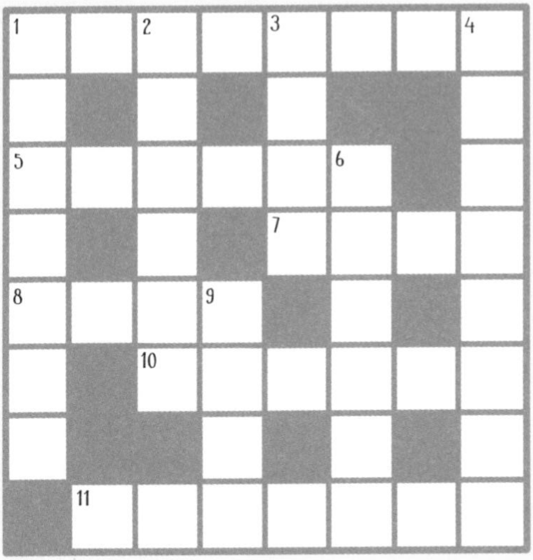

62

1		2		3			4
5					6		
				7			
8			9				
		10					
	11						

ACROSS

1. Very short candle in a metal cup (8)
5. Apart from (6)
7. In *Star Wars*, the arch-enemies of the Jedi (4)
8. Paper-thin metal sheet (4)
10. Your aunt and uncle's child (6)
11. Chuckles (7)

DOWN

1. _______ Night, the end of the Christmas season, when all decorations are taken down; also a play by William Shakespeare (7)
2. Region around the North Pole (6)
3. Little goblins (4)
4. US actor who voiced Woody in *Toy Story*, and starred in *Turner & Hooch* (3, 5)
6. Glittering, metallic Christmas decoration (6)
9. Lengthy (4)

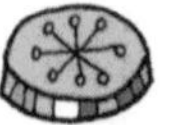

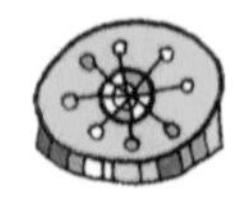

ACROSS

1. Large sock left out for Santa (8)
5. Uprising, public disturbance (4)
7. Note added at the end of a letter (1.1.)
8. Put numbers together (3)
10. Tidy (4)
12. Little pictures you can attach to things (8)

DOWN

2. Spinning toys (4)
3. You might leave one out for Santa's reindeer on Christmas Eve (6)
4. This divides a tennis court (3)
6. Sweet citrus fruit (6)
7. Frogs lay their eggs in these (5)
9. Hounds (4)
11. Muhammad ___, US boxing champion who died in 2016 (3)

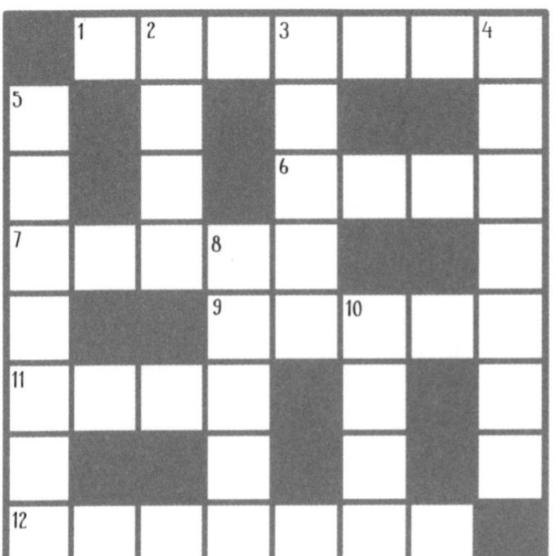

ACROSS

1. It makes a high-pitched sound when you blow it (7)
6. ____ years have 366 days (4)
7. Chocolate ones are often eaten at Christmas (5)
9. Bird of prey (5)
11. Pulls another vehicle behind it (4)
12. Women's garments (7)

DOWN

2. Stereo music system (2-2)
3. Chunky tomato dip; Latin dance (5)
4. *The Polar* _______, Christmas movie about a train to the North Pole (7)
5. Eager, looking forward to something (7)
8. Where birds lay eggs (5)
10. Sticky stuff (4)

ACROSS

1. Light gusts of snow (8)
5. Clint _________, US star of westerns, and movie director (8)
7. Frozen blocks that drift at sea (8)
9. Getting, acquiring (7)

DOWN

1. Extremely cold (8)
2. Risky, hazardous (6)
3. Uncooked (3)
4. Sorrow (7)
6. Move faster than (6)
8. Make illegal (3)

ACROSS

1. Snowstorm (8)
5. Camel-like South American animals (6)
7. Water dripping where it shouldn't (4)
8. Lose footing on a smooth surface (4)
10. Wolf-like North American animal (6)
11. You wear these to keep the sides of your head warm (8)

DOWN

1. The middle of a target (5, 3)
2. Slanted type *like this* (6)
3. Enthusiasm, gusto (4)
4. Night, gloom (8)
6. Begin a journey (3, 3)
9. *Jabberwocky*, for example (4)

67

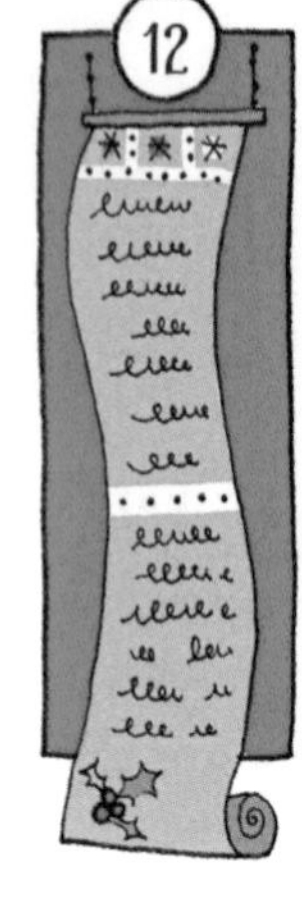

ACROSS

1. Advent ________, Christmas countdown, often with chocolates (8)
5. Tropical lizards (6)
7. Embrace (3)
8. What you shout when you jump out to scare someone (3)
9. Awe, amazement (6)
12. Record of the gifts you'd like (4, 4)

DOWN

1. Clockwork wheel (3)
2. Large deer (3)
3. Sprinted (6)
4. What you do with a bell (4)
6. Masses of people (6)
8. Prepare tea or coffee (4)
10. Zero points (3)
11. Large rodent (3)

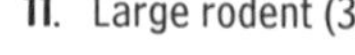

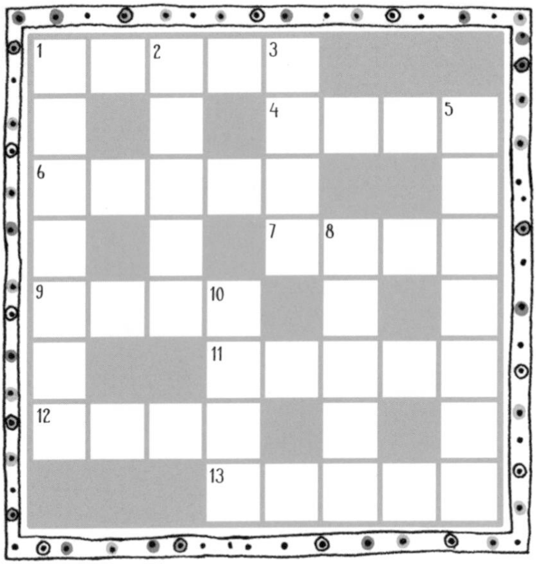

1		2		3	■	■	■
	■		■	4			5
6					■	■	
	■		■	7	8		
9			10	■		■	
	■	■	11				
12				■		■	
■	■	■	13				

ACROSS

1. Pop or jazz, for example (5)
4. Your parent's sister (4)
6. Have faith in, rely on (5)
7. Many deserts are covered in this (4)
9. At any time (4)
11. Piano-like instrument often found in churches (5)
12. Han ____, Chewbacca's best friend in *Star Wars* (4)
13. Senses, touches (5)

DOWN

1. Gloves without fingers (7)
2. Dressing, relish (5)
3. They are said to have nine lives (4)
5. "Glad _______ we bring, to you and your king!" (7)
8. Disagree, fight (5)
10. House covering (4)

1		2			3		4
				5			
6			7				
			8		9		
10		11			12		
13							

ACROSS

1. Saint ________, another name for Santa Claus (8)
5. The number of suits in a deck of cards (4)
6. More (5)
8. Gobbled up (3)
10. Noise of a cannon (4)
12. A sawn-off section of tree-trunk (3)
13. These animals help Santa get around (8)

DOWN

1. The eleventh month (8)
2. Two-wheeled vehicle pulled by an animal (4)
3. The star sign of the Lion (3)
4. Unfamiliar person (8)
5. Overweight (3)
7. Butt, crash into (3)
9. "It's not mine – it belongs to someone ____." (4)
11. ___-Wan Kenobi, Jedi Master (3)

70

1		2		3			4
	■		■		■	■	
5					6	■	
	■		■	7			
8			9	■		■	
	■	10					
	■	■		■		■	
11							

ACROSS

1. Giving, big-hearted (8)
5. Santa's flying vehicle (6)
7. You use this for washing (4)
8. The ____ Sisters made Cinderella's life miserable (4)
10. The continent that Poland and Greece belong to (6)
11. Some person (8)

DOWN

1. Hand movements that say something (8)
2. You use this for sewing (6)
3. Old pieces of cloth (4)
4. Hard to grasp (8)
6. Santa's famous booming laugh (2, 2, 2)
9. Old name for the Christmas season (4)

71

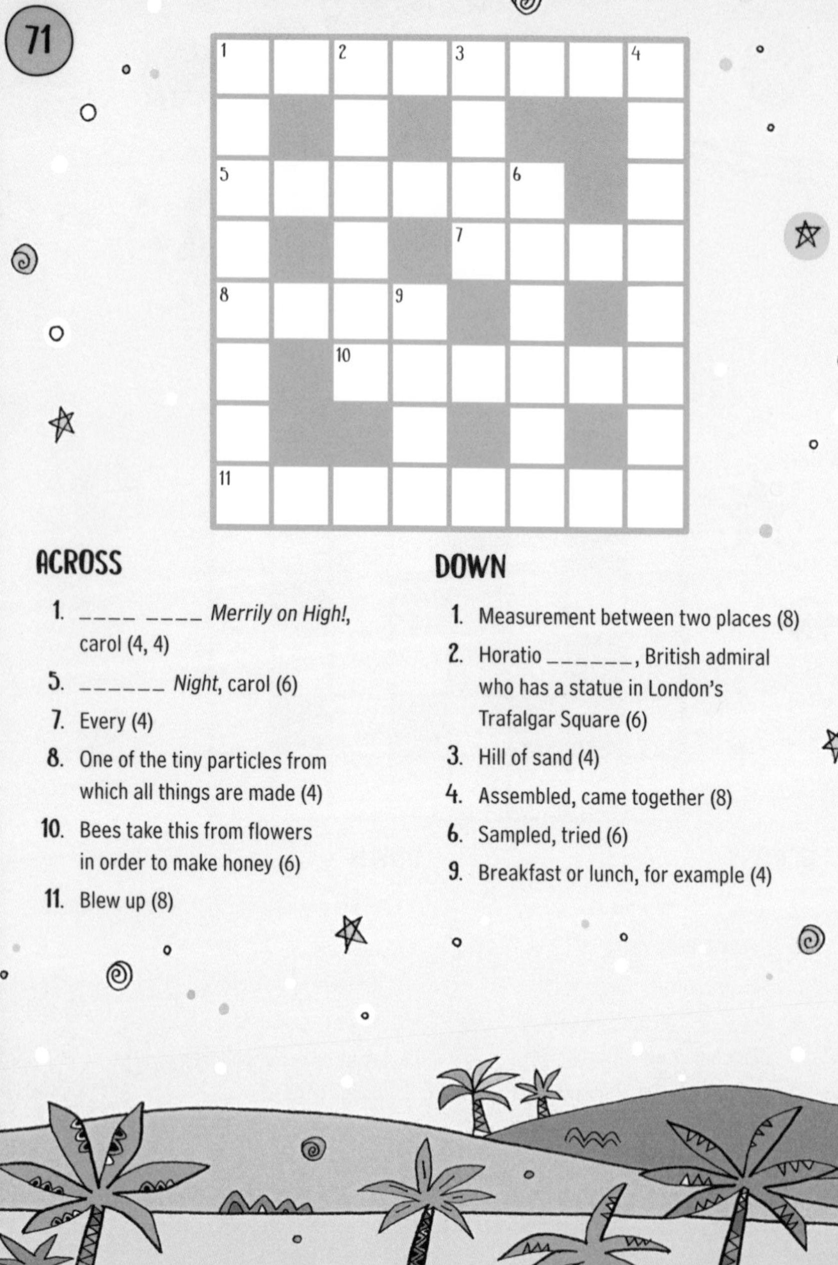

ACROSS

1. ____ ____ *Merrily on High!*, carol (4, 4)
5. ______ *Night*, carol (6)
7. Every (4)
8. One of the tiny particles from which all things are made (4)
10. Bees take this from flowers in order to make honey (6)
11. Blew up (8)

DOWN

1. Measurement between two places (8)
2. Horatio ______, British admiral who has a statue in London's Trafalgar Square (6)
3. Hill of sand (4)
4. Assembled, came together (8)
6. Sampled, tried (6)
9. Breakfast or lunch, for example (4)

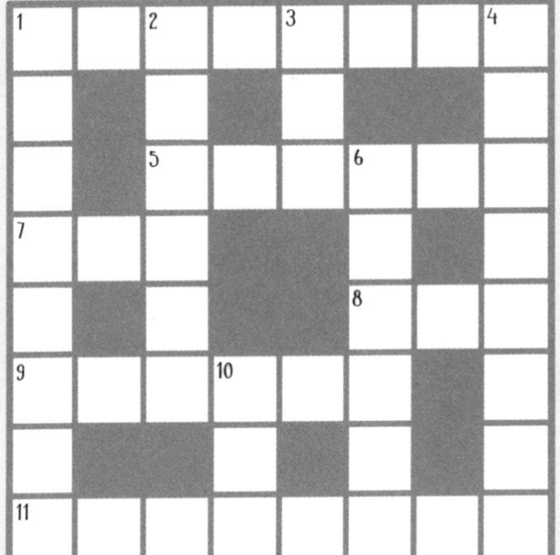

ACROSS

1. *Go, Tell it on the ________*, carol (8)
5. Mel ______, US actor (6)
7. Stick used in pool or snooker (3)
8. French for "street" (3)
9. *O ______ Town of Bethlehem*, carol (6)
11. Reply, reaction (8)

DOWN

1. Beefy, well-built (8)
2. Important to deal with immediately (6)
3. Bath (3)
4. If I said that pigs can fly, I would be talking ________ (8)
6. Monitor, display (6)
10. Hit lightly (3)

ACROSS

1. Crescent-shaped nut (6)
6. Also known as (1.1.1.)
7. Violent, savage (6)
9. ___ Flanders lives next door to Homer Simpson (3)
10. How pirates say "yes" (3)
11. Someone who suffers from an accident or crime (6)
14. Short for "I have" (3)
15. Bite off small pieces (6)

DOWN

2. Gas you breathe (3)
3. Successful song (3)
4. Nut with a wrinkled shell (6)
5. Happening by chance (6)
7. This nut comes from South America's largest country (6)
8. Rough, not level (6)
12. Taxi (3)
13. ___ *be home for Christmas*, seasonal song (3)

1		2		3			4
	■		■		■	■	
5					6	■	
	■		■	7			
8			9	■		■	
	■	10					
	■	■		■		■	
11							■

ACROSS

1. This little, round nut grows in Europe, Asia, and in the USA where it's also known as a filbert (8)
5. Area, province (6)
7. The one after this (4)
8. Shut a door hard (4)
10. Rule over, run (6)
11. These nuts are often served salted (7)

DOWN

1. Difficulty, trouble (8)
2. Jagged line (6)
3. Big cat with a mane (4)
4. Checking, examining (7)
6. Most recent (6)
9. "The Man in the ____ came down too soon..." (4)

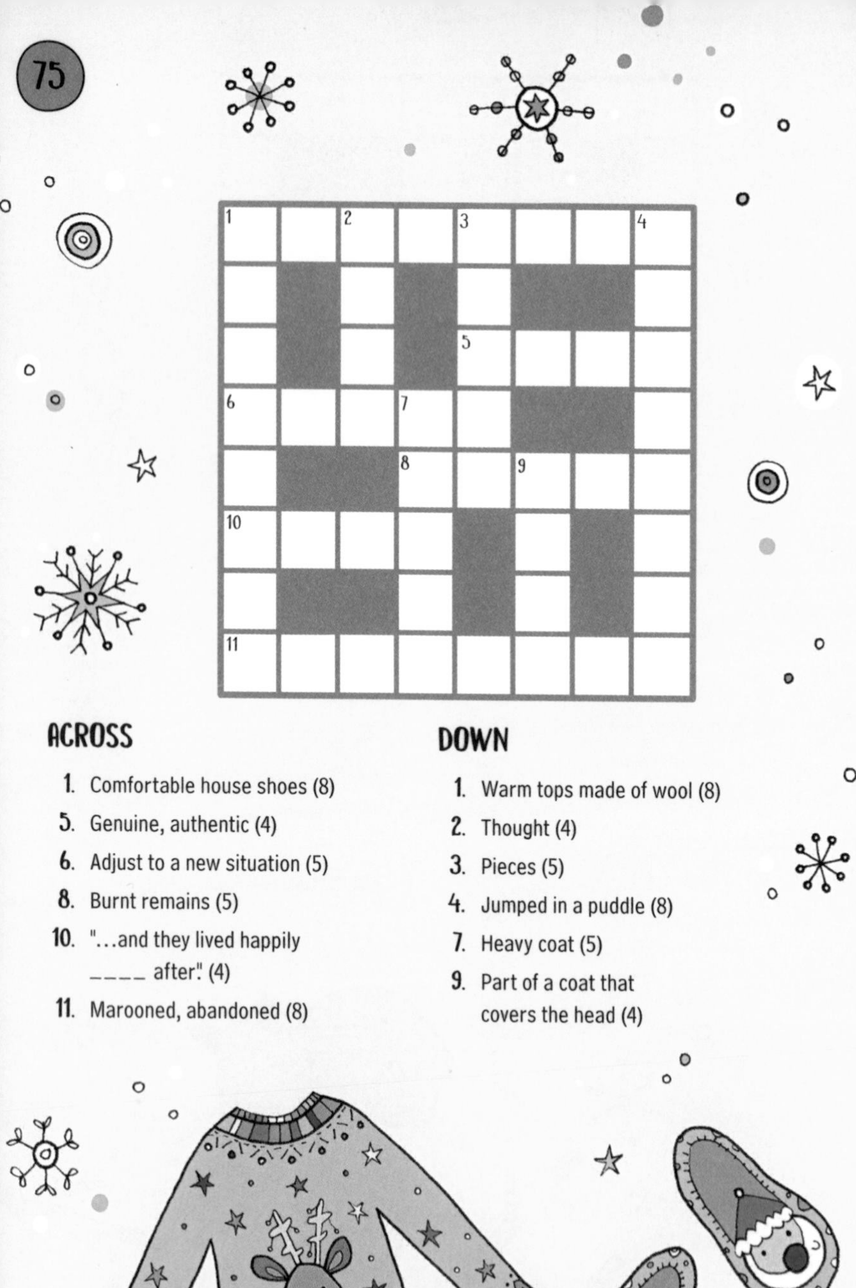

ACROSS

1. Comfortable house shoes (8)
5. Genuine, authentic (4)
6. Adjust to a new situation (5)
8. Burnt remains (5)
10. "...and they lived happily ____ after." (4)
11. Marooned, abandoned (8)

DOWN

1. Warm tops made of wool (8)
2. Thought (4)
3. Pieces (5)
4. Jumped in a puddle (8)
7. Heavy coat (5)
9. Part of a coat that covers the head (4)

1			2		3		4
	■	■		■		■	
5						■	
	■	■		■	6		
7		8	■	9	■	■	
	■	10					
	■		■		■	■	
11							■

ACROSS

1. Warm, open-fronted top with buttons (8)
5. Light wind (6)
6. Soggy (3)
7. "A long time ___" (3)
10. Type of flatfish (6)
11. Wise king in the Bible (7)

DOWN

1. Green, leafy vegetables (8)
2. Nancy ____, girl detective (4)
3. Got bigger (4)
4. "She is _______ tall nor short." (7)
8. Rainbow gemstone (4)
9. Toasty (4)

1			2		3		
		4					5
6							
				7			
8							
		9					

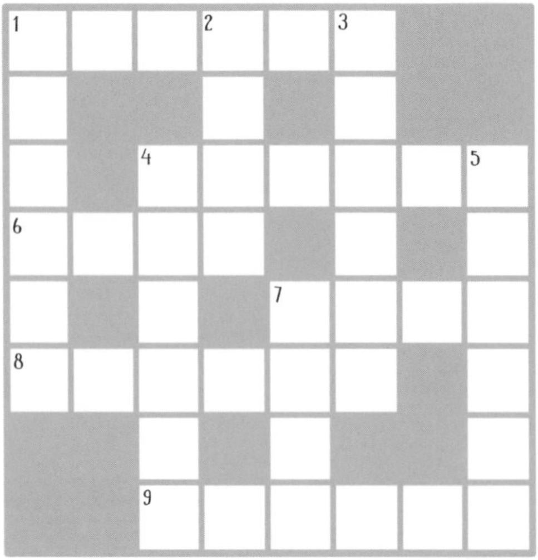

ACROSS

1. Santa's ______, cavern-like space at a department store where children can meet the Man in Red (6)
4. Prickly desert plant (6)
6. First word in a letter (4)
7. Clock or watch face (4)
8. When someone is feeling festive, you say they are full of Christmas ______ (6)
9. Collect (6)

DOWN

1. Forest clearings (6)
2. Drop of sadness (4)
3. Set of clothes (6)
4. Kind, compassionate (6)
5. Precious metal (6)
7. Soil (4)

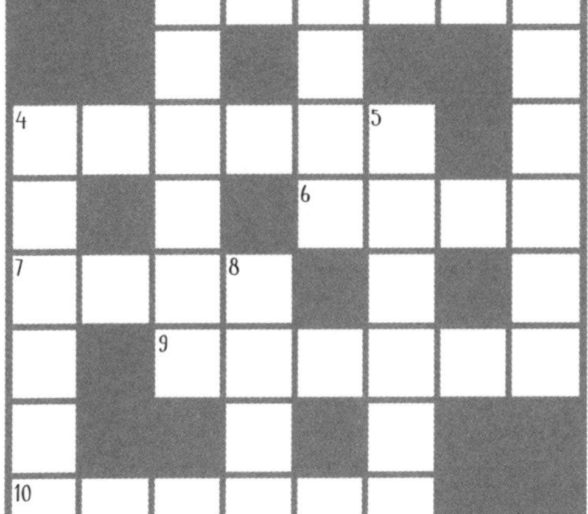

ACROSS

1. ______ Christmas, another name for Santa Claus (6)
4. Mountain peak (6)
6. Departed (4)
7. Small room for a prisoner or a monk (4)
9. Made a tired sound (6)
10. Gratitude (6)

DOWN

1. Closest relatives (6)
2. A dog wags it (4)
3. Relaxed (6)
4. Piece of knowledge you keep to yourself (6)
5. Racket sport (6)
8. Grassy area by a house (4)

ACROSS

1. Play about the birth of Jesus (8)
5. Animal feeding trough in which the baby Jesus was laid (6)
8. The noise a snake makes (4)
11. Temporary shelter (4)
14. Animal shed (6)
17. More brilliant (8)

DOWN

1. The noise a horse makes (5)
2. Trains a wild animal to be a pet (5)
3. Vincent ___ Gogh, Dutch artist (3)
4. You have one big one on each foot (3)
6. Obtained (3)
7. Move quickly (3)
9. Belonging to it (3)
10. The Red, Black or Caspian, for example (3)
12. Throw or shoot out (5)
13. Striped big cat (5)
15. Sticky, black substance (3)
16. Insect (3)

1		2		3		4		5
						6		
7								
8					9			
				10				
				11				12
13								
		14						

ACROSS

1. The angel who told Mary that she would give birth to Jesus (7)
6. Mary and Joseph stayed in a stable because there was no room at the ___ (3)
7. The _____ of the Boy Scouts is "Be prepared." (5)
8. Aid, assistance (4)
9. Celebrity (4)
11. Blood vessels (5)
13. Fearful wonder (3)
14. Coped, ran, led (7)

DOWN

1. Something you chew but don't swallow (3)
2. The town where Jesus was born (9)
3. Common metal (4)
4. Often goes with thunder (9)
5. Fury (5)
8. Person, *Homo sapiens* (5)
10. Opposite of odd (4)
12. Unhappy (3)

ACROSS

1. Leafy, ring-shaped decoration (6)
5. A playing card (3)
6. Sides, limits (5)
8. American relative of the crocodile (9)
10. Creepy, spooky (5)
12. Ask strangers for money (3)
13. Soft, squashy washing-aid (6)

DOWN

1. A unicycle has just one (5)
2. This word describes trees that keep their leaves in winter (9)
3. Pull (3)
4. Royal home (6)
7. Small bunches of leaves (6)
9. King Arthur and the Knights of the Round _____ (5)
11. Tear (3)

ACROSS

1. Prickly green tree with red berries, used for Christmas decoration (5)
6. Opponent, foe (5)
7. Plant with white berries under which people kiss at Christmas (9)
10. Fine hairs that protect your vision (9)
15. Someone who doesn't eat meat or 11 down, and tries to avoid all animal products (5)
16. Book of maps (5)

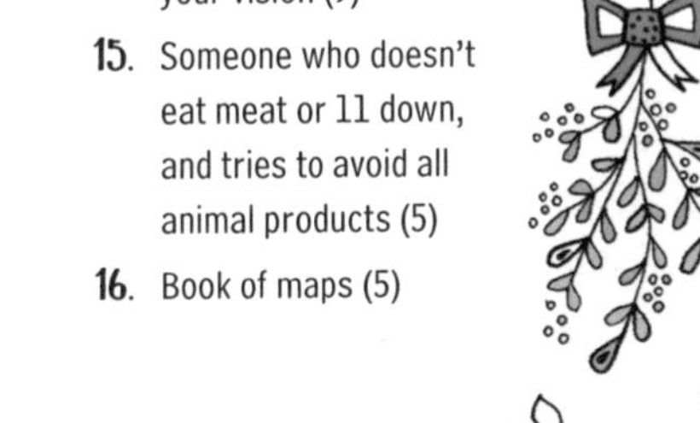

DOWN

1. Hurt, damage (4)
2. A spider has eight (4)
3. Shout (4)
4. Cried (4)
5. Use a keyboard (4)
8. Common, leafy plant that climbs up walls and houses (3)
9. 7÷7 (3)
10. Jealousy (4)
11. Birds lay these (4)
12. Elsa's sister in *Frozen* (4)
13. Cure (4)
14. Cries loudly (4)

ACROSS

1. Writing tools (4)
4. Large farm bird often roasted for Christmas or Thanksgiving dinner (6)
6. Grassy soil (4)
7. Quick (4)
9. Bad cold (3)
10. Indian silk outfit (4)
12. Herb often used with onion to season 2 down; wise person (4)
13. St. George killed one (6)
14. Chess or hopscotch, for example (4)

DOWN

1. Dinner is served on these (6)
2. A 4 across is often filled with this herby, breadcrumb mixture (8)
3. Stories of the day on TV or radio (4)
5. Saying no, declining (8)
8. How many hours are there on a clock face? (6)
11. Unit of land area roughly equal to the size of a football field (4)

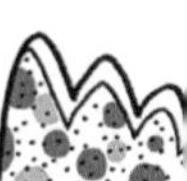

ACROSS

1. These are often served roasted or mashed for Christmas dinner (8)
6. Male sheep (3)
7. Occur again (5)
8. Organ of smell (4)
9. Rules (4)
12. Location, spot (5)
14. Consumed (3)
15. Twitchy, fidgety (8)

DOWN

1. Sweet, white root vegetables (8)
2. Three _____ three is nine (5)
3. Open pie (4)
4. Short for *et cetera* (3)
5. ________ sprouts – small vegetables that take their name from the capital of Belgium (8)
10. Not asleep (5)
11. Opposite of right (4)
13. "Two heads ___ better than one." (3)

1		2	■	3		4		5
	■		■		■		■	
6					■	7		
	■	■	■		■		■	■
8		9						10
■	■		■		■	■	■	
11			■	12		13		
	■		■		■		■	
14					■	15		

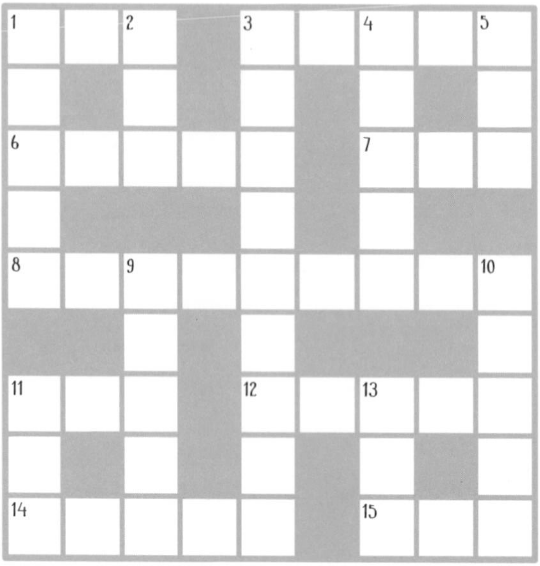

ACROSS

1. Toss, throw (3)
3. Amazing, tremendous (5)
6. Seat (5)
7. Fitting, appropriate (3)
8. In the ballet *The Nutcracker*, the _____ ____ Fairy is the ruler of the Land of Sweets (5, 4)
11. Yellow and black buzzing insect (3)
12. Serpent (5)
14. Jotted down (5)
15. Title for a married woman (3)

DOWN

1. Keys go into these (5)
2. The sound a sheep makes (3)
3. Startled (9)
4. Precious stone found in oyster shells (5)
5. Decay (3)
9. The _____ Wall of China (5)
10. Encounters (5)
11. Big ___, London clocktower (3)
13. Point towards a target (3)

86

1		2		3		4		5
	■		■		■		■	
6			■		■	7		
	■	■	■		■	■	■	
8		9				10		
■	■		■		■		■	■
11			12		13			14
	■	■	15			■	■	
16				■	17			

ACROSS

1. Rodent-catching device (9)
6. ___ de Janeiro, big city in Brazil (3)
7. Expected to arrive (3)
8. Stargazing instrument (9)
11. This word describes machines that work by themselves (9)
15. Marry (3)
16. Murder (4)
17. This is used to season food (4)

DOWN

1. Deserve, earn (5)
2. Flying saucer (1.1.1.)
3. Polite phrase when you wish to move past someone (6, 2)
4. When you get ___ of something, you throw it away (3)
5. Part (5)
9. Set on fire, ignited (3)
10. Opposite of in (3)
11. *Raiders of the Lost ___* (3)
12. Hooting bird (3)
13. Short for advertisements (3)
14. Small wound (3)

1				2	■	3		4
	■	■	■		■		■	
5		6					■	
■	■		■		■		■	
7								
	■		■		■		■	■
	■	8						9
	■		■		■	■	■	
10			■	11				

ACROSS

1. Loft (5)
3. Not many (3)
5. Large, hairy tropical nut with sweet white flesh and milk (7)
7. Fruit chew in the shape of a honey-loving wild animal (5, 4)
8. Groups of students (7)
10. Text-speak for Laugh Out Loud (1.1.1.)
11. Like, take pleasure in (5)

DOWN

1. Curve (3)
2. This Christmas treat has red and white stripes (5, 4)
3. Health and strength (7)
4. Clear liquid (5)
6. Funny (7)
7. Barbecue (5)
9. Dark, salty Chinese sauce (3)

ACROSS

1. _______ delight – sweet, rose-scented treat from an eastern country (7)
5. Do something (3)
7. Comes into view (7)
8. This soft, sweet, creamy treat comes in many varieties, such as vanilla, chocolate and nut (5)
9. The UK's fighting plane division (1.1.1.)
10. Sob (3)
12. Defy, fight back (5)
13. Nose holes (8)

DOWN

1. Flow of vehicles (7)
2. Quickly (7)
3. Picture (5)
4. Owns (3)
6. Soft, buttery chocolates, often dusted with cocoa powder (8)
9. Jewish religious teacher (5)
11. Sprint (3)
12. Groove, furrow (3)

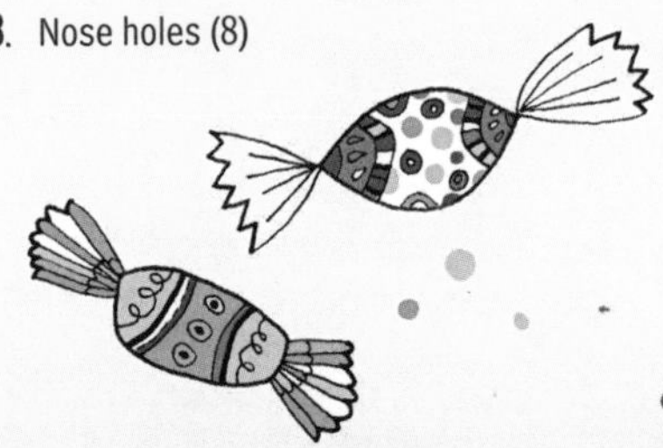

ACROSS

1. Straw roof covering on old houses (6)
4. Clumsy fool (3)
6. Make someone feel better (7)
7. Twist or roll up into a circle (4)
9. Treble ____, twirly symbol at the start of a piece of music (4)
10. Santa gets into a house down one of these (7)
12. Common tree (3)
13. Doze (6)

DOWN

1. Ten divided by five (3)
2. Terrible (5)
3. Place to stay when you're away (5)
5. Soft, fuzzy (6)
6. This bird might pop out of a clock (6)
8. Big stones (5)
9. Short for combination (5)
11. The Cyclops only had one (3)

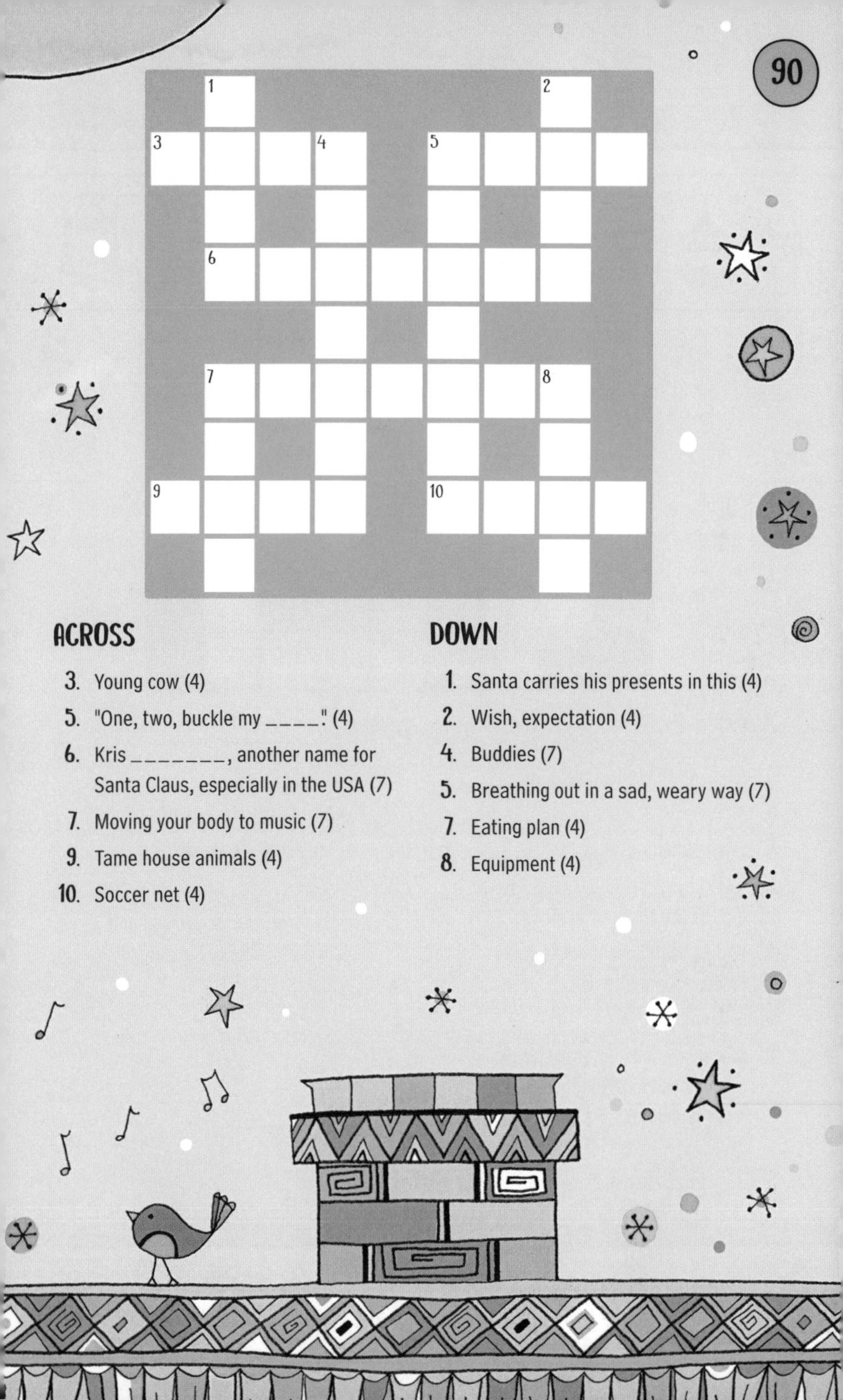

ACROSS

3. Young cow (4)
5. "One, two, buckle my ____." (4)
6. Kris _______, another name for Santa Claus, especially in the USA (7)
7. Moving your body to music (7)
9. Tame house animals (4)
10. Soccer net (4)

DOWN

1. Santa carries his presents in this (4)
2. Wish, expectation (4)
4. Buddies (7)
5. Breathing out in a sad, weary way (7)
7. Eating plan (4)
8. Equipment (4)

91

ACROSS

1. Mixture, confusion, mess (6)
4. Alphabet (1.1.1.)
6. Unkind, mean (5)
7. "Good King _________ looked out, on the Feast of Stephen…" (9)
9. Little pictures you click to open an app or program (5)
11. Hideout, lair (3)
12. Sweet, creamy Christmas drink, enjoyed especially in the USA and Canada (6)

DOWN

1. Glass pot (3)
2. Trusting, having faith in (9)
3. Painter's wooden stand (5)
5. Shuts (6)
6. Someone who lacks courage and runs from trouble or danger (6)
8. Nobody (2, 3)
10. Pester (3)

ACROSS

2. Company that works for good causes (7)
5. Unmarried woman who lives in a religious community (3)
6. Donald J. _____ was elected US President in 2016 (5)
8. This goes around your waist (4)
9. The largest continent (4)
12. She was married to Charles, Prince of Wales, and died tragically in 1997 (5)
14. Through (3)
15. Repeating design (7)

DOWN

1. Double-decker sleeping platform (4, 3)
2. Man-made waterway (5)
3. Little insects (4)
4. Note to show you owe money (1.1.1.)
7. Common farm worker in the Middle Ages (7)
10. How many "seas" are there traditionally said to be? (5)
11. Sheet of paper in a book (4)
13. Painting or sculpture, for example (3)

ACROSS

1. Pale brown spice added to cakes and desserts, and sprinkled over hot drinks (8)
5. Inhabited, or in use (8)
7. Rabbits have long ones (4)
9. Old wound (4)
11. Building with sails (8)
12. Herb with needle-like leaves; also a girl's name (8)

DOWN

1. These dried flowerbuds from a tropical tree make a strong, warming spice (6)
2. More pleasant (5)
3. "...with silver bells and cockleshells and pretty _____ all in a row" (5)
4. " ___ off" means fall asleep (3)
6. Lacy, fancy (6)
8. Musical pieces with words (5)
10. Pottery (5)
11. Armed conflict (3)

ACROSS

1. This spice is added to milky desserts and hot drinks (6)
4. Opposite of young (3)
6. Breaststroke and butterfly are two ways to do this (4)
7. "I beg your ______?" (6)
9. Fruit such as oranges, lemons and limes (6)
11. Shape with six square faces (4)
13. A knight's title (3)
14. 30 x 3 (6)

DOWN

1. At the present time (3)
2. If you suddenly get angry, you are said to have lost your ______ (6)
3. Virtuous, kind, well-behaved (4)
5. Hang, suspend (6)
6. Pieces of tree branch (6)
8. Save from danger (6)
10. Change direction (4)
12. Young male (3)

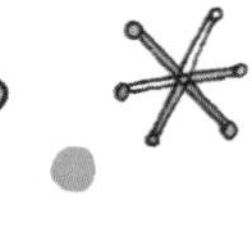

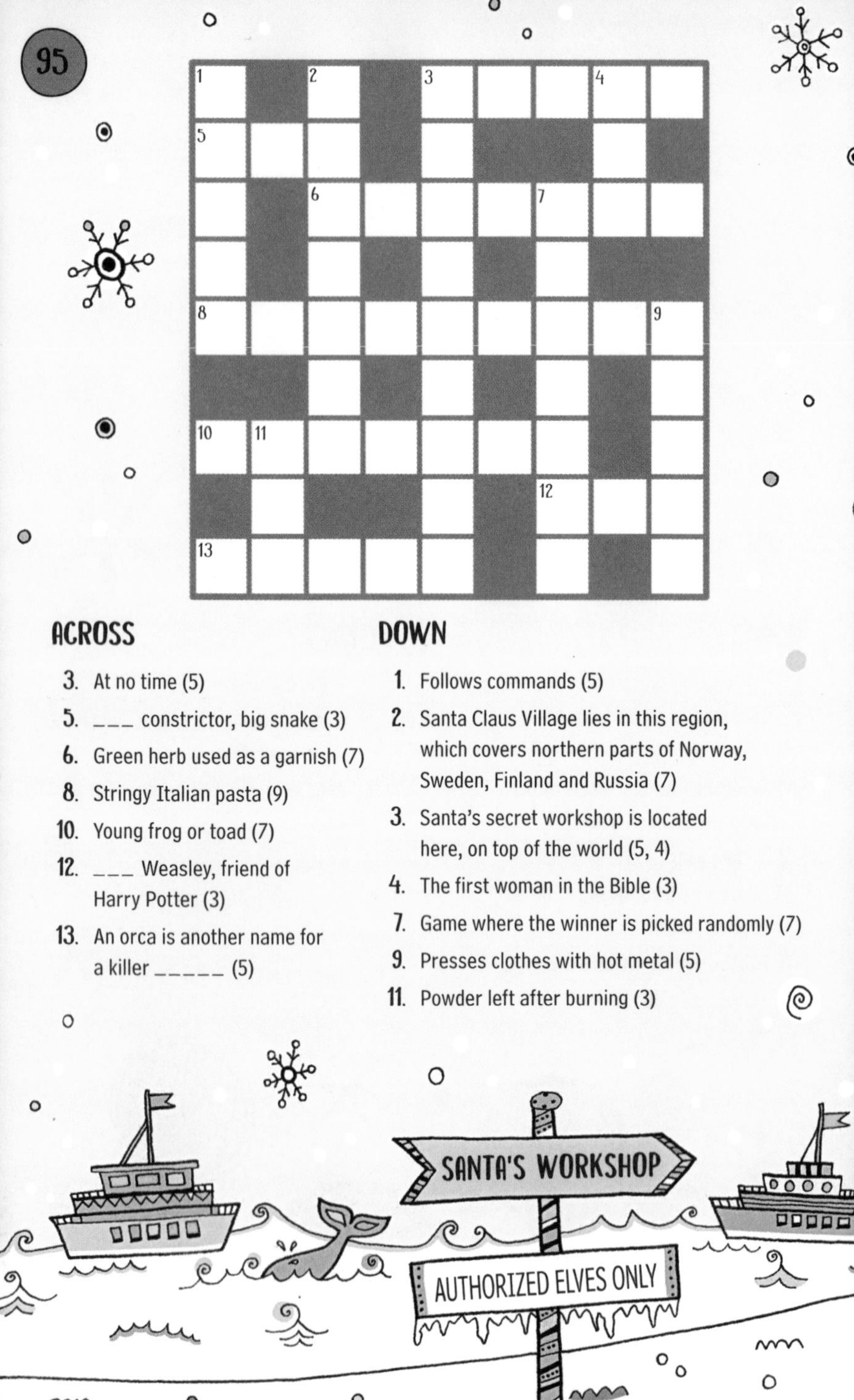

ACROSS

3. At no time (5)
5. ___ constrictor, big snake (3)
6. Green herb used as a garnish (7)
8. Stringy Italian pasta (9)
10. Young frog or toad (7)
12. ___ Weasley, friend of Harry Potter (3)
13. An orca is another name for a killer _____ (5)

DOWN

1. Follows commands (5)
2. Santa Claus Village lies in this region, which covers northern parts of Norway, Sweden, Finland and Russia (7)
3. Santa's secret workshop is located here, on top of the world (5, 4)
4. The first woman in the Bible (3)
7. Game where the winner is picked randomly (7)
9. Presses clothes with hot metal (5)
11. Powder left after burning (3)

ACROSS

1. Santa's little helpers (5)
4. Purpose, goal (3)
6. Cut grass (3)
7. The lead character in the Christmas movie *Elf*, played by Will Ferrell (5)
8. Large, white Arctic animal (5, 4)
10. Subject, theme (5)
12. Little spot (3)
14. Shack (3)
15. Sweet pouring sauce (5)

DOWN

1. Tall tree (3)
2. "A" or "E", for example (5)
3. Takes away (9)
4. & (3)
5. Town or city leader (5)
8. Piece of material used to cover a tear or hole (5)
9. The oldest of two people (5)
11. Light touch with the palm or fingers (3)
13. Push over (3)

ACROSS

1. "_________ roasting on an open fire..." (9)
5. Chocolate powder, or the hot drink it's used to make (5)
7. Fuzzy fabric (4)
8. Leg joint (4)
9. "____ as a bug in a rug" (4)
11. Explosive device (4)
13. Hold-up, interruption (5)
14. Harmful to eat or drink (9)

DOWN

1. End of a shirt-sleeve (4)
2. Freckle, mark (4)
3. Alcove, corner (4)
4. Protected from harm (4)
5. Rain falls from this (5)
6. Irritate (5)
9. Liquid meal (4)
10. Jewels (4)
11. Farm building (4)
12. Flying night animals (4)

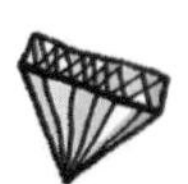

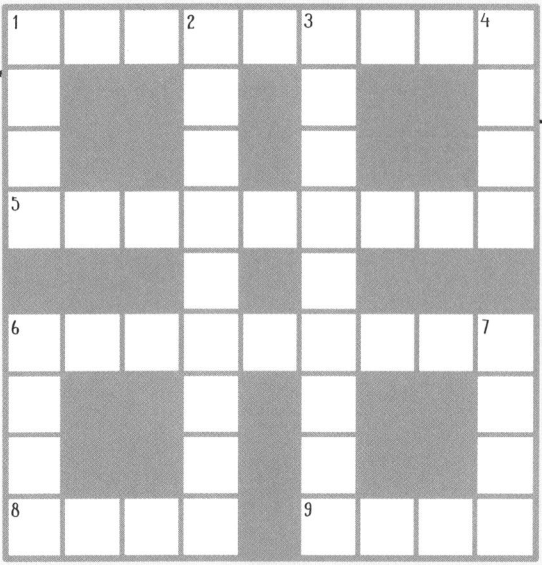

98

1			2		3			4
	■	■		■		■	■	
	■	■		■		■	■	
5								
■	■	■		■		■	■	■
6								7
	■	■		■		■	■	
	■	■		■		■	■	
8				■	9			

ACROSS

1. December 25th (9)
5. Chance meeting (9)
6. Hearth (9)
8. Strong affection (4)
9. Wide smile (4)

DOWN

1. Hole in the rocks (4)
2. Opposite of guilt (9)
3. Flickering like a star (9)
4. Fly high (4)
6. Brimming (4)
7. Make money (4)

1		2			3			
							4	
5			6		7			
8	9							10
11					12	13		
			14					

ACROSS

1. Haven, safe place (6)
5. Pig meat (4)
7. Scheme, design (4)
8. These grow on evergreen trees (4, 5)
11. Tumble (4)
12. Sound that bounces back (4)
14. ______ spruce, this evergreen tree shares its name with the Scandinavian country that sends a huge one to London and Washington DC each Christmas (6)

DOWN

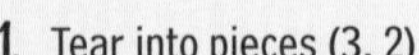

1. Tear into pieces (3, 2)

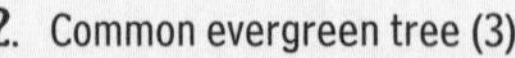

2. Common evergreen tree (3)
3. Look around a new area (7)
4. Fierce wind (4)
6. HQ of the Russian government (7)
9. Middle Eastern country bordering Iran, its capital is Baghdad (4)
10. Tintin’s little white dog (5)
13. Farm animal kept mainly for milk (3)

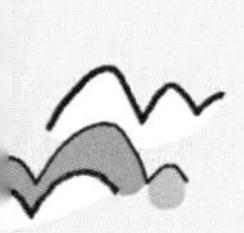

ACROSS

2. Cone-bearing tree (7)
5. Be in debt (3)
6. Made up your mind (7)
8. Health resort (3)
9. Sweet-smelling flowers (5)
11. Flat-faced dog (3)
12. Upper or outer part (7)
14. Girl's name (3)
15. Rotted, crumbled (7)

DOWN

1. The solid remains of long-dead creatures (7)
2. Type of 2 across (5)
3. Needed, essential (9)
4. Craze, trend (3)
7. _______ fir, very tall North American tree that has a Scottish boy's name (7)
10. How fast something is going (5)
13. Giant bird met by Sindbad the sailor on one of his voyages (3)

101

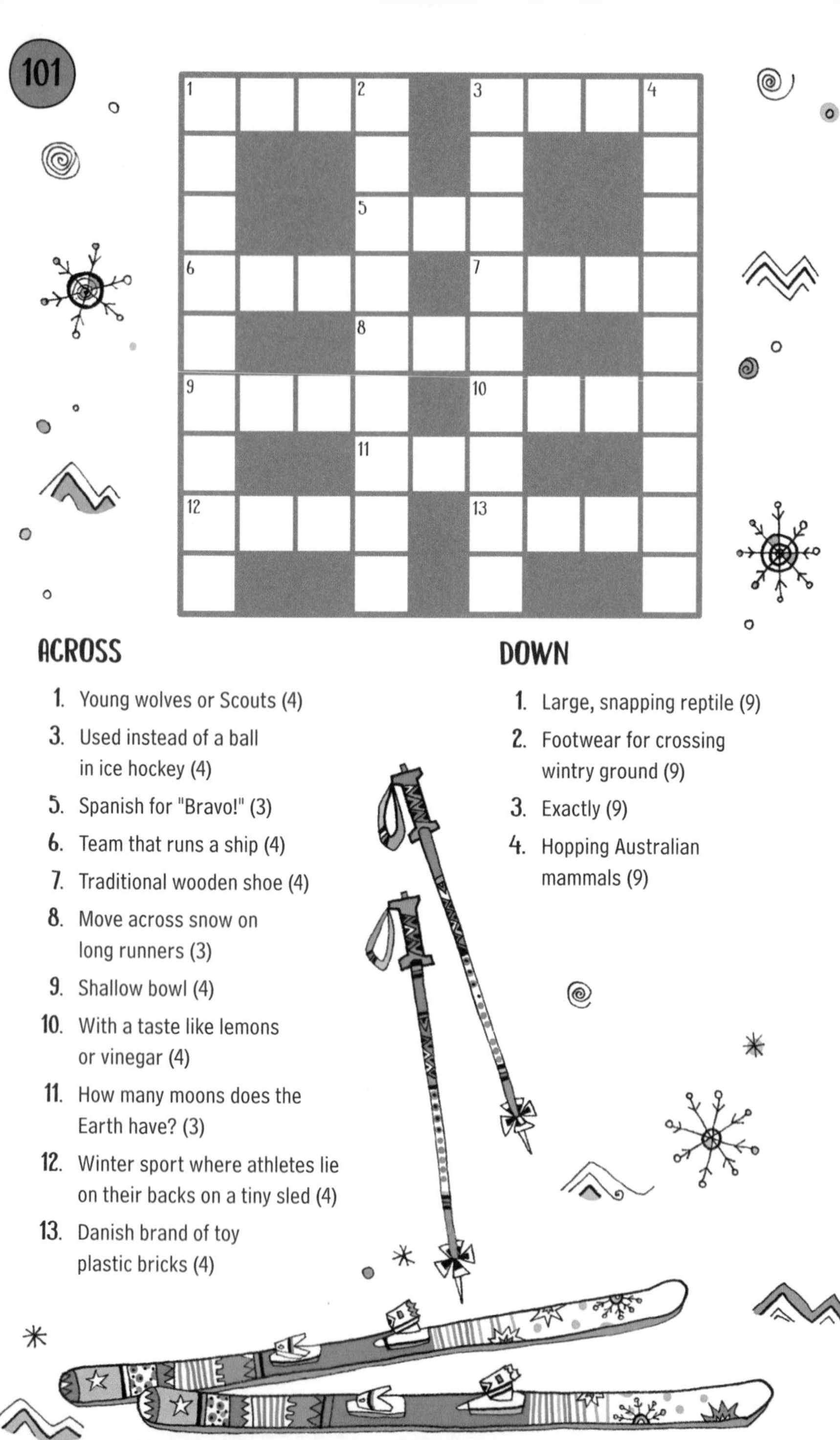

ACROSS

1. Young wolves or Scouts (4)
3. Used instead of a ball in ice hockey (4)
5. Spanish for "Bravo!" (3)
6. Team that runs a ship (4)
7. Traditional wooden shoe (4)
8. Move across snow on long runners (3)
9. Shallow bowl (4)
10. With a taste like lemons or vinegar (4)
11. How many moons does the Earth have? (3)
12. Winter sport where athletes lie on their backs on a tiny sled (4)
13. Danish brand of toy plastic bricks (4)

DOWN

1. Large, snapping reptile (9)
2. Footwear for crossing wintry ground (9)
3. Exactly (9)
4. Hopping Australian mammals (9)

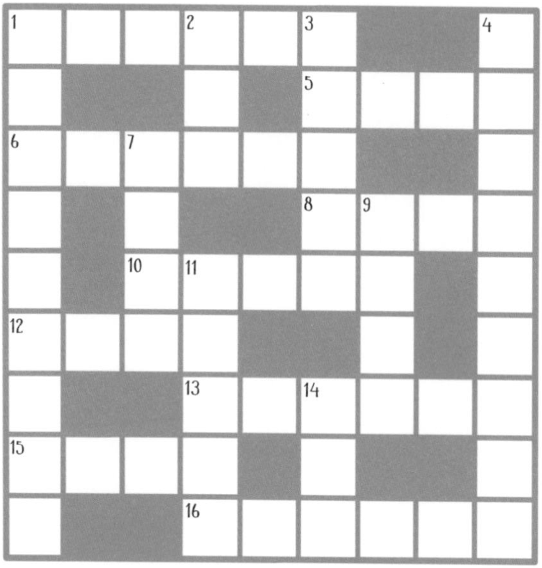

1			2		3	■	■	4
	■	■		■	5			
6		7				■	■	
	■		■	■	8	9		
	■	10	11				■	
12				■	■		■	
	■	■	13		14			
15				■		■	■	
	■	■	16					

ACROSS

1. Ski race that zigzags around flags (6)
5. Large Middle Eastern country that used to be known as Persia (4)
6. Insult, anger (6)
8. Play or musical (4)
10. Texas or Oklahoma, for example (5)
12. Solemn vow (4)
13. "A friend in need is a friend ______." (6)
15. Uncommon (4)
16. ______ skating, Olympic sport which includes ice dancing (6)

DOWN

1. You ride this in a winter sport (9)
2. Christopher ___, British actor who died in 2015, famed for playing Count Dracula and the wizard Saruman (3)
3. Old-fashioned word for "middle" (5)
4. What a person has learned (9)
7. Clenched hand (4)
9. In this place (4)
11. Robber (5)
14. Use a shovel (3)

103

ACROSS

1. Burrowing animal with large claws and a black-and-white-striped face (6)
5. Gorillas or chimpanzees, for example (4)
6. Doze through the winter, as some animals do (9)
9. A way of serving eggs by mixing them up in a pan (9)
13. Going down a long way (4)
14. Wave rider (6)

DOWN

1. Leafy, trunkless plant (4)
2. Entrance in a fence (4)
3. Wet weather (4)
4. Common insect (6)
7. There are 12 in a foot (6)
8. Lip, edge (3)
10. Europe's longest mountain range (4)
11. Wild pig (4)
12. Animals with hooves and antlers (4)

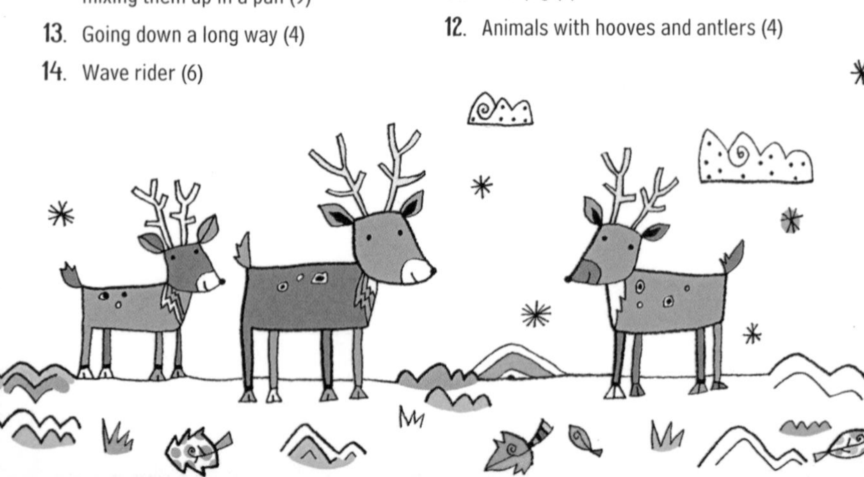

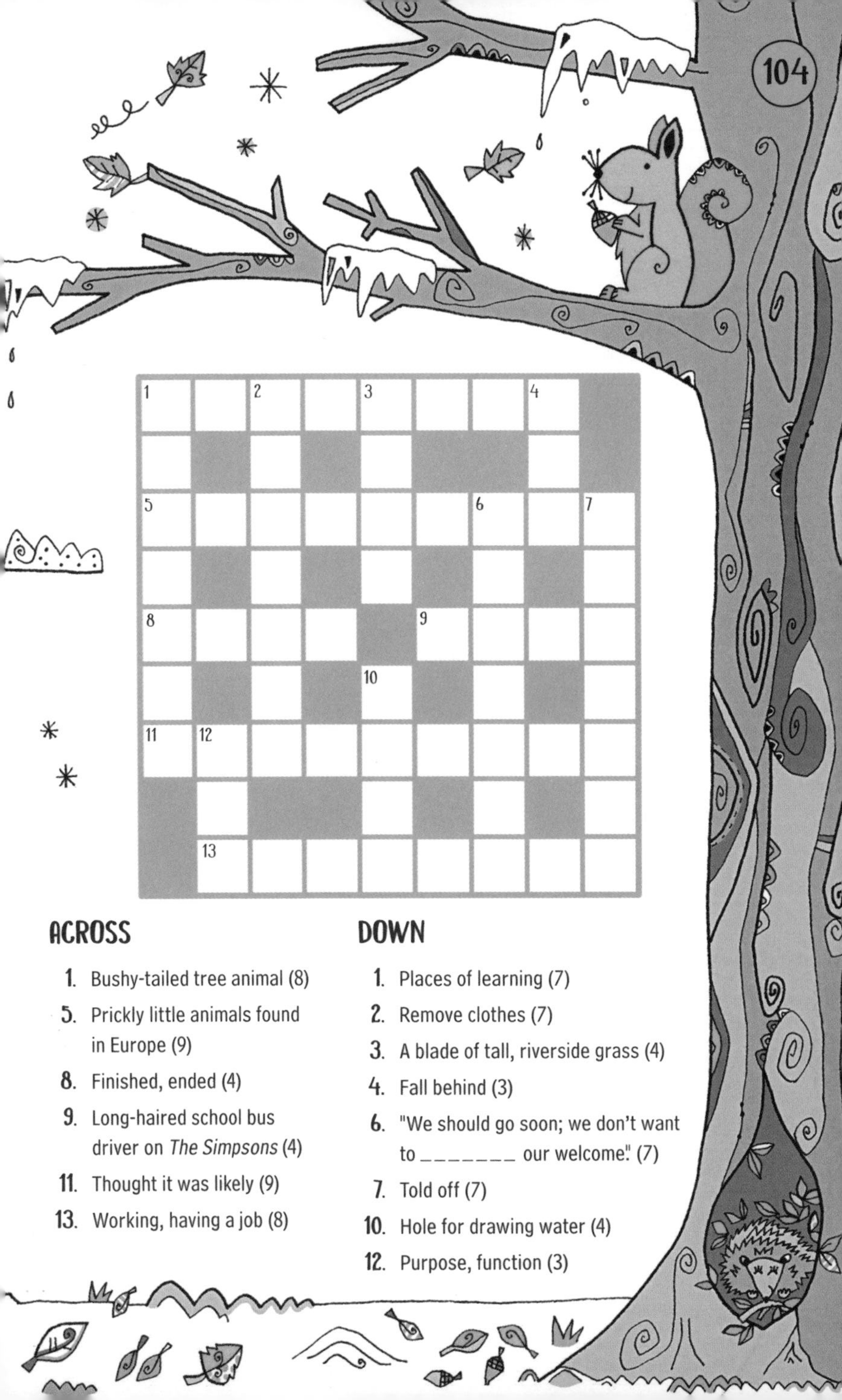

ACROSS

1. Bushy-tailed tree animal (8)
5. Prickly little animals found in Europe (9)
8. Finished, ended (4)
9. Long-haired school bus driver on *The Simpsons* (4)
11. Thought it was likely (9)
13. Working, having a job (8)

DOWN

1. Places of learning (7)
2. Remove clothes (7)
3. A blade of tall, riverside grass (4)
4. Fall behind (3)
6. "We should go soon; we don't want to _______ our welcome." (7)
7. Told off (7)
10. Hole for drawing water (4)
12. Purpose, function (3)

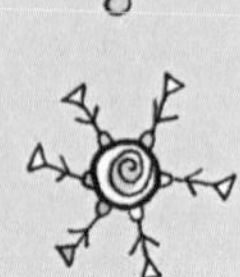

1	■	2			3		4	
5			■	■		■		■
	■		■	6				7
8			■		■	■	■	
	■	9				10	■	
	■	■	■		■	11		
12	13		14		■		■	
■		■		■	■	15		
16							■	

ACROSS

2. (with 6 down) British actor who played Ebenezer Scrooge in *The Muppet Christmas Carol* (7, 5)
5. Japanese carp (3)
6. Wept (5)
8. Golfball stand (3)
9. Crumbling old buildings (5)
11. Deep Chinese frying pan (3)
12. Spinning model of the Earth (5)
15. Very heavy weight (3)
16. Stone or bronze models of people or animals (7)

DOWN

1. Sliding across ice in special boots (7)
2. Mean, stingy person (5)
3. "Grace shook ___ head." (3)
4. Female sheep (3)
6. (See 2 across)
7. Charles _______, author of *A Christmas Carol* (7)
10. Hits a fly (5)
13. Allow (3)
14. Except (3)

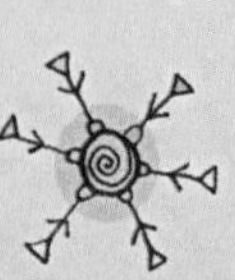

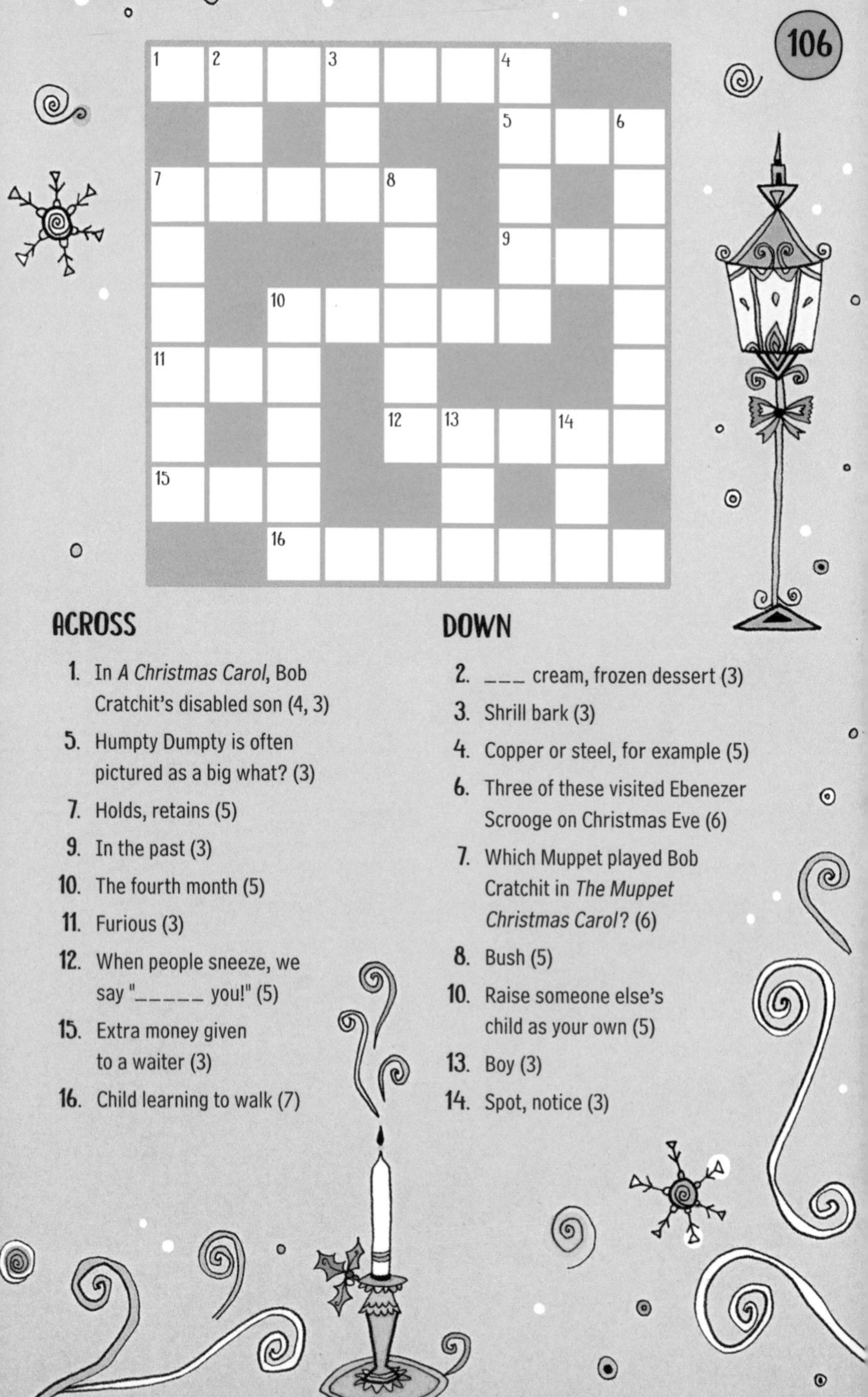

ACROSS

1. In *A Christmas Carol*, Bob Cratchit's disabled son (4, 3)
5. Humpty Dumpty is often pictured as a big what? (3)
7. Holds, retains (5)
9. In the past (3)
10. The fourth month (5)
11. Furious (3)
12. When people sneeze, we say "_____ you!" (5)
15. Extra money given to a waiter (3)
16. Child learning to walk (7)

DOWN

2. ___ cream, frozen dessert (3)
3. Shrill bark (3)
4. Copper or steel, for example (5)
6. Three of these visited Ebenezer Scrooge on Christmas Eve (6)
7. Which Muppet played Bob Cratchit in *The Muppet Christmas Carol*? (6)
8. Bush (5)
10. Raise someone else's child as your own (5)
13. Boy (3)
14. Spot, notice (3)

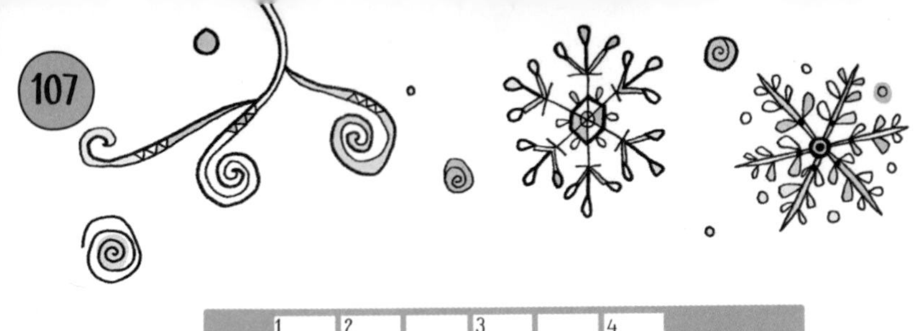

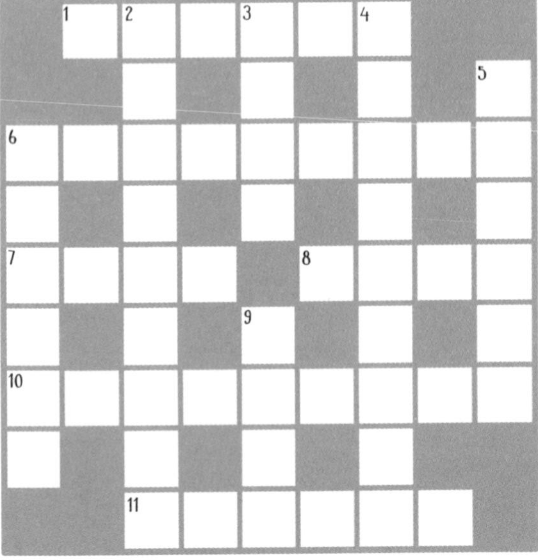

ACROSS

1. Frightens (6)
6. Magical sprite said to paint windows with swirling, icy patterns (4, 5)
7. Hair-grooming tool (4)
8. Title of former Russian rulers (4)
10. All the people (9)
11. Plan, plot (6)

DOWN

2. Long, green salad vegetables (9)
3. Simple wooden boat (4)
4. Blizzard (9)
5. Solid, robust (6)
6. Short coat (6)
9. Ancient story of gods and heroes (4)

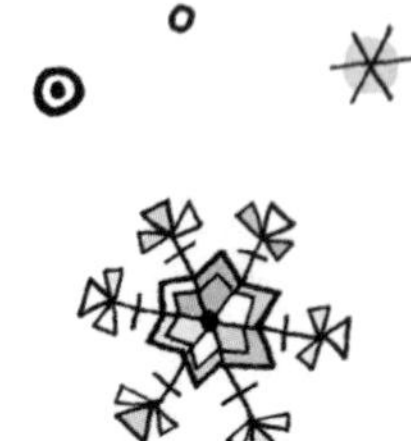

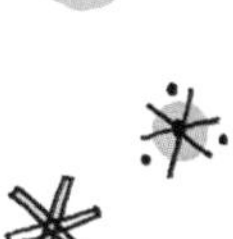

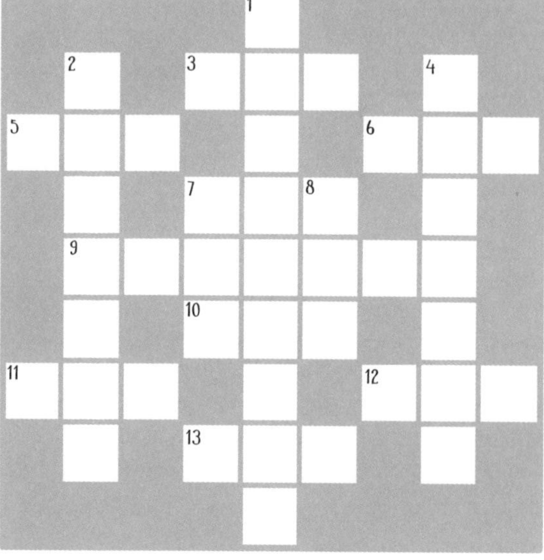

ACROSS

3. Dark liquid squirted out by squid (3)
5. Waterless (3)
6. How many sides does a hexagon have? (3)
7. 8 ÷ 4 (3)
9. Smelled (7)
10. Magical, pointy-eared being (3)
11. Item of headwear (3)
12. Fresh, novel (3)
13. It is above the Earth (3)

DOWN

1. Tiny white thing that floats down from the sky when it's cold (9)
2. Very fine, clear glass (7)
4. Puzzling questions (7)
7. Bind (3)
8. The opposite of "on" (3)

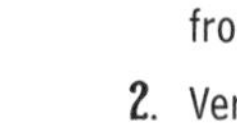

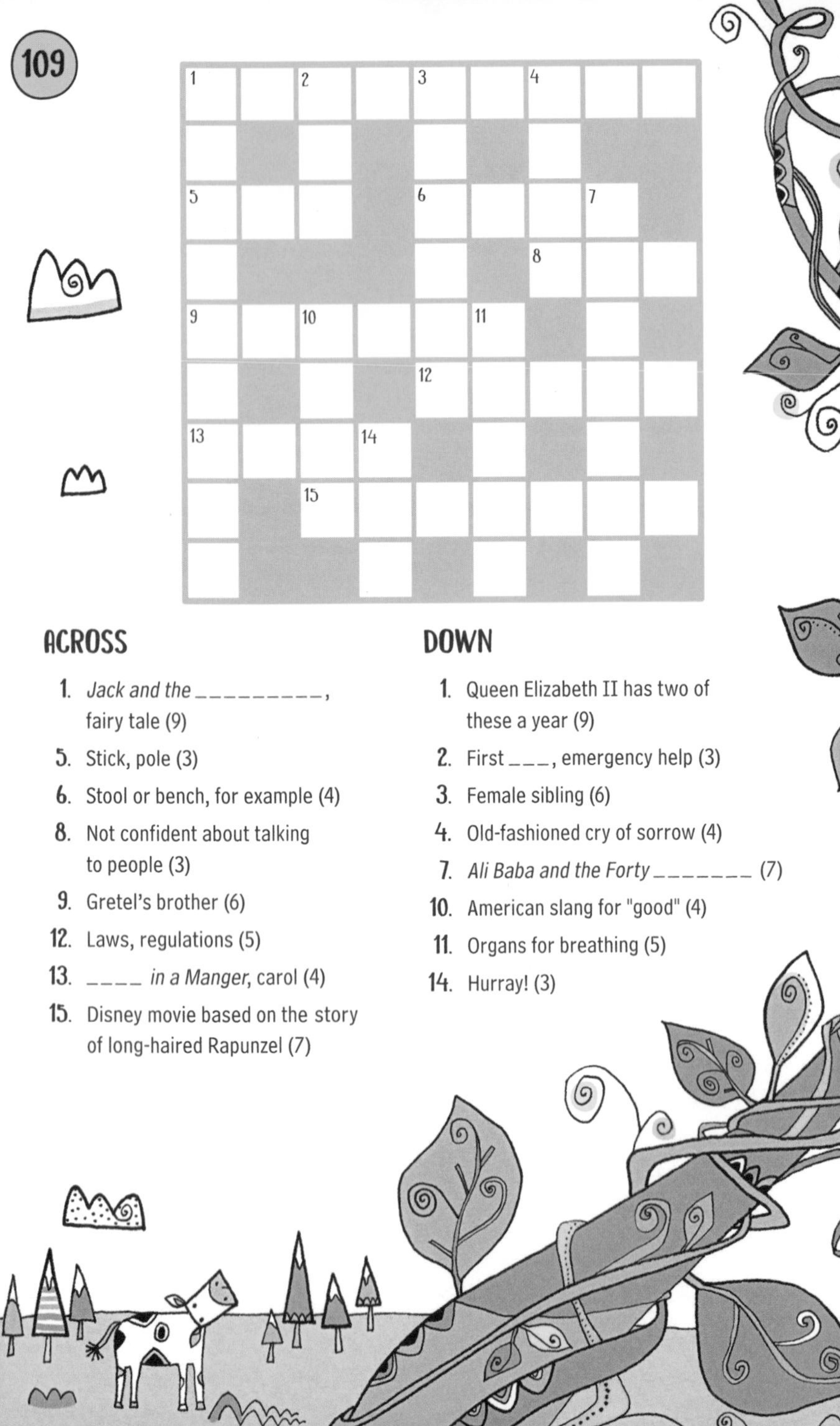

ACROSS

1. *Jack and the* _________, fairy tale (9)
5. Stick, pole (3)
6. Stool or bench, for example (4)
8. Not confident about talking to people (3)
9. Gretel's brother (6)
12. Laws, regulations (5)
13. ____ *in a Manger*, carol (4)
15. Disney movie based on the story of long-haired Rapunzel (7)

DOWN

1. Queen Elizabeth II has two of these a year (9)
2. First ___, emergency help (3)
3. Female sibling (6)
4. Old-fashioned cry of sorrow (4)
7. *Ali Baba and the Forty* _______ (7)
10. American slang for "good" (4)
11. Organs for breathing (5)
14. Hurray! (3)

ACROSS

1. Make a tune with your mouth shut (3)
3. Gemstone (5)
6. (with 7 across) *Little* ___ ______ ____, fairy tale about a girl, her grandmother, and a wolf (3, 6, 4)
7. (see 6 across)
9. Cow meat (4)
12. Legendary outlaw of Sherwood Forest (5, 4)
14. Soak in a tub (5)
15. Top, cap (3)

DOWN

1. Stern, cruel (5)
2. Wet soil (3)
3. Prison (4)
4. *Snow _____ and the Seven Dwarfs* (5)
5. Lower limb (3)
8. Path circling a star or planet (5)
10. Dimmed, died away (5)
11. " ____ upon a time..." (4)
12. Stroke, massage (3)
13. Black liquid fuel (3)

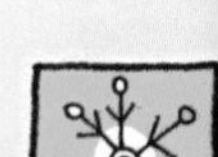

ACROSS

1. Mobile game released in 2016 that allows you to catch cartoon monsters out and about in the real world (7, 2)
6. Regularly (5)
7. You wipe your feet on this (3)
8. Workouts (9)
11. Earl Grey, for example (3)
12. In front (5)
14. Animals (9)

DOWN

1. Confirm with evidence (5)
2. Set of equipment (3)
3. Video game where you can build anything out of blocks (9)
4. What you call people by (5)
5. Choose (3)
9. Remove, rub out (5)
10. A square has four (5)
11. Facial twitch (3)
13. Spike of corn (3)

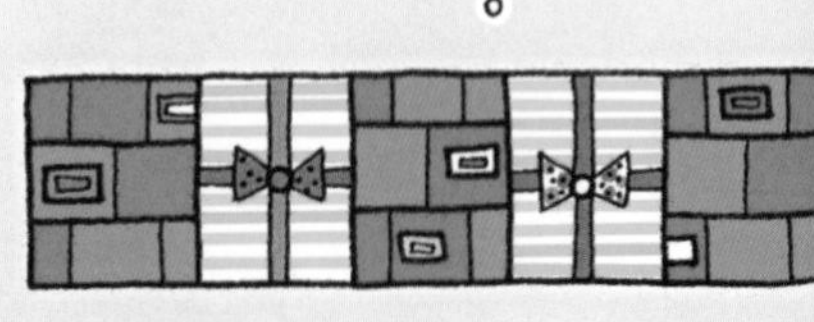

ACROSS

1. Heroine of *Tomb Raider* (4, 5)
6. Notebook (3)
7. Italian plumber who stars in a video game with his brother, Luigi (5)
8. Cease (4)
9. Having the power to do something (4)
12. Opposite of south (5)
14. Small carpet (3)
16. Owned up, admitted (9)

DOWN

1. You only have one when you sit down (3)
2. Machine that plays music and talk shows (5)
3. Approach (4)
4. Belonging to us (3)
5. "Not these but _____" (5)
8. _____ *the Hedgehog*, video game (5)
10. *Angry* _____, mobile game (5)
11. You may cry this as you go down a slide (4)
13. Hurried (3)
15. Divine being (3)

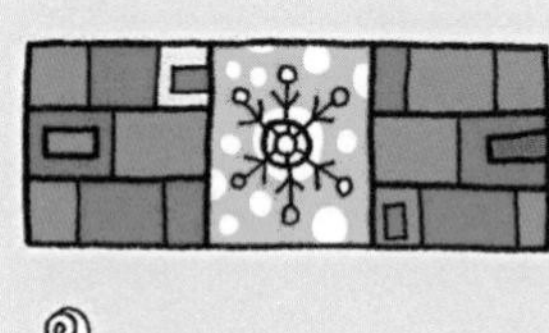

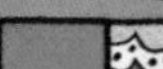

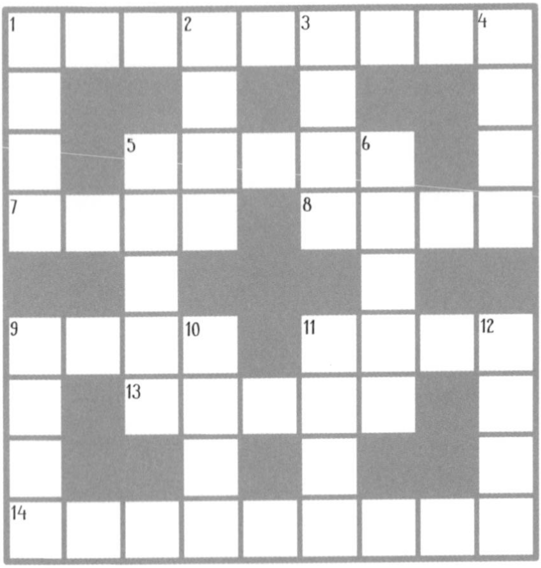

1			2		3			4
	■	■		■		■	■	
	■	5				6	■	
7				■	8			
■	■		■	■	■		■	■
9			10	■	11			12
	■	13					■	
	■	■		■		■	■	
14								

ACROSS

1. You might throw these in a fun winter fight (9)
5. Go and see; call upon (5)
7. Make out of wool (4)
8. Squishy (4)
9. Move your foot forward (4)
11. Creamed potato (4)
13. Bellybutton (5)
14. Thankfulness (9)

DOWN

1. You wear this on your foot (4)
2. Hang around (4)
3. The line around which something spins (4)
4. Closed (4)
5. A female fox; one of Santa's reindeer (5)
6. Final sum (5)
9. Adult male deer (4)
10. Time gone by (4)
11. What all snowmen must do eventually (4)
12. Where you live (4)

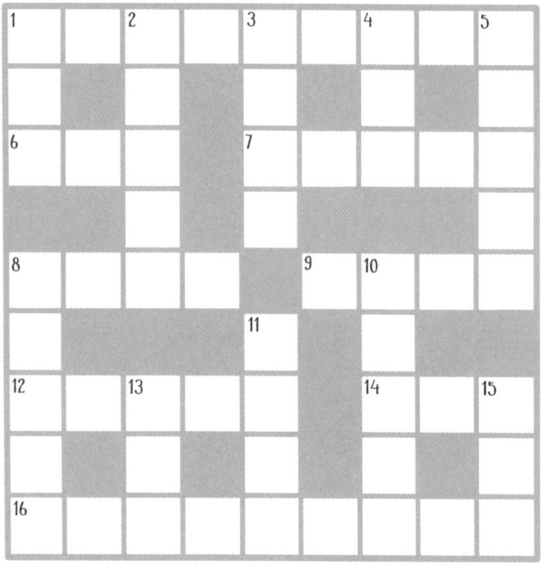

1		2		3		4		5
	■		■		■		■	
6			■	7				
■	■		■		■	■	■	
8				■	9	10		
	■	■	■	11	■		■	■
12		13			■	14		15
	■		■		■		■	
16								

ACROSS

1. On December 27th, this is 16 across (6, 3)
6. American spy agency that works all around the world (1.1.1.)
7. Black and white bear (5)
8. Skip a question (4)
9. The Red Planet (4)
12. Contact sport where you can run with the ball in hand (5)
14. Program on a mobile device (3)
16. The day before today (9)

DOWN

1. Britain's national TV and radio service (1.1.1.)
2. Invisible beams used by doctors to see inside your body (1-4)
3. Bites or pinches (4)
4. Racket, commotion (3)
5. There are 100 in a century (5)
8. Celebration (5)
10. Prize (5)
11. Sort, kind (4)
13. Helium or methane, for example (3)
15. Give money in return for something (3)

ACROSS

6. & 7. Glass sphere holding water and a winter scene (4, 5)
8. Event, occurrence (8)
9. Celebration meal (5)
11. Splendid, impressive (5)
14. Simple drawing of a person (5, 3)
17. Coming from the area nearby (5)
18. Stretched circle (4)

DOWN

1. Tip, point (3)
2. Dangling seats found in playgrounds (6)
3. One more time (5)
4. Capital of Italy (4)
5. Isaac ______, English scientist who discovered gravity, born on Christmas Day 1642 (6)
10. Simply (6)
12. Motive, cause (6)
13. Talent (5)
15. Empire that once ruled Peru (4)
16. Meat often eaten at Christmas (3)

ACROSS

1. *The ______*, sci-fi movie starring Keanu Reeves (6)
4. Short for Christmas (4)
8. Annoy, frustrate (3)
9. Instance, illustration (7)
10. Male cows (5)
11. Mobile message (4)
15. Superhero team led by Professor Charles Xavier (1-3)
16. Precise (5)
19. Time between afternoon and night (7)
21. Cunning, sneaky (3)
22. Short name for the world's most famous scary dinosaur (1. 3)
23. Used by both boys and girls, for example, a changing room (6)

DOWN

1. Change position (4)
2. Feel of a surface (7)
3. Principles, beliefs (6)
5. Floor-washing tool (3)
6. You put these on a bed (6)
7. Money people pay to the government to pay for things like roads and schools (3)
12. Reasons given for not doing something (7)
13. Specialist, master (6)
14. Gas that we need to breathe (6)
17. Combine, stir (3)
18. Tufty-eared, bob-tailed wildcat (4)
20. The London ___, Ferris wheel on the bank of the River Thames (3)

1
MERRY
A O O
GROWL
I T K
CAST

2
BELLS
I A L
ROUTE
T G E
H HOP

3
TRAIN
O M I
YOUNG
S S H
WEST

4
HOBBY
O A O
RELAY
S L O
EASY

5
TEDDY
A R E
BEARS
B M
YEARN

6
BARKS
U O H
COBRA
K O R
SIT P

7
T
COATS
L N T
ANKLE
M S W

8
NIPPY
O I E
EIGHT
L G I
GYM

9
MAYBE
N O
IGLOO
L T
BEAST

10
LIGHT
A A A
MAZES
B E K
ODD

11
F
HILLS
A O A
LUCKY
O K S

12
PEACE
I B A
CHOIR
K V T
YEAH

13
G
BIRDS
A A I
GIVEN
S Y G

14
GOOSE
U V N
EVENT
S N R
TASTY

15
SWANS
I G T
THREE
E E E
PEAR

16
TOWN
E H
NOISY
T O
MENU

17
S A B
HOUSE
I L L
PEDAL
S Y

18
SHOUT
N W R
OUNCE
W E E
FRY

19
ACORN
N P I
GREEN
E R E
LEAF

20
BOUGH
U N E
SHINE
Y T L
EYES

21
GIFTS
L A E
OLIVE
W T M
WHO

22
CARDS
L O C
UPON O
E MESS
S E T
HIDES

23
RIBBON
U O E
SLOW A
S ISNT
I L L
ANYWAY

24
POST T
A AHA
WRAP G
I GETS
SEE E
H STAY

25
WINTER
O E V
O CHEW
LIKE A
C A V
PEOPLE

26
FIRE H
R LIE
OATS A
Z HALT
ERA E
N WEAR

27
ICICLE
C O D
E BLOW
AGED A
G S R
EXTEND

28
CAMELS
R I C
O STAR
WISE O
N N L
SANDAL

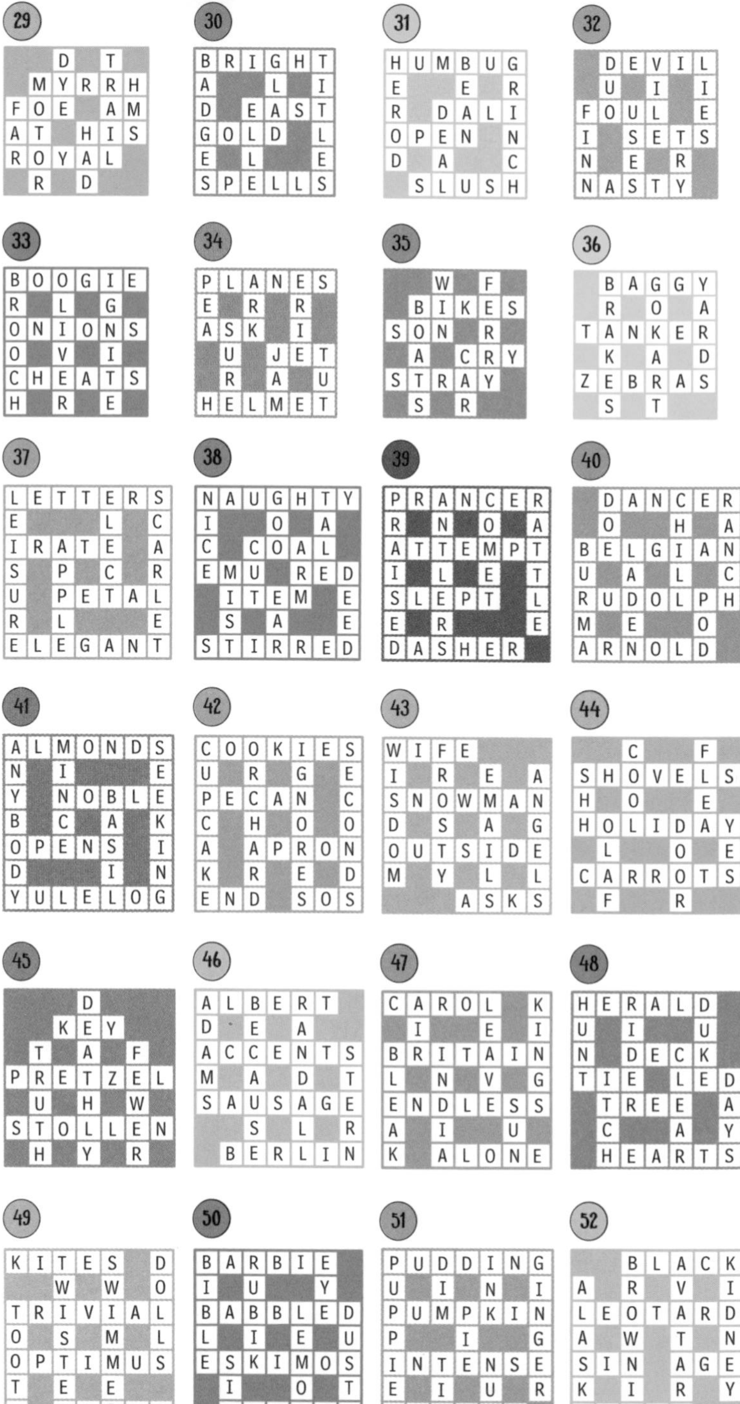

53

			H			
		F	E	E		
	C	O	M	M	A	
P		U		P		I
A	N	G	R	I	E	R
R		H		R		I
K	I	T	T	E	N	S

54

B	I	G		P	A	W
U		A		A		E
M	I	R	A	C	L	E
P		D		K		K
	B	E	R	E	T	
		N	O	D		
			W			

55

B	U	B	B	L	E	
A		A		A		
T	A	L	C	U	M	
H		A		G		C
	A	N	C	H	O	R
		C		E		O
	M	E	A	D	O	W

56

P	E	R	F	U	M	E
A			E		O	
S	H	A	M	P	O	O
T			A			G
E	A	R	L	I	E	R
	C		E			E
S	T	A	S	H	E	S

57

D	I	P	S		A	
A			K	I	N	D
W			I		N	
N	E	E	D	L	E	S
	V		D			P
P	I	L	E			A
	L		D	R	U	M

58

P	U	D	D	L	E	
U		E		I		
F	R	E	E	Z	E	
F		P		A		F
	S	P	I	R	A	L
		A		D		E
	U	N	U	S	E	D

59

D	U	M	M	Y		
U		U		E		
C	A	P		T	I	P
K		P				U
S	W	E	E	T	E	N
		T		O		C
		S	L	O	T	H

60

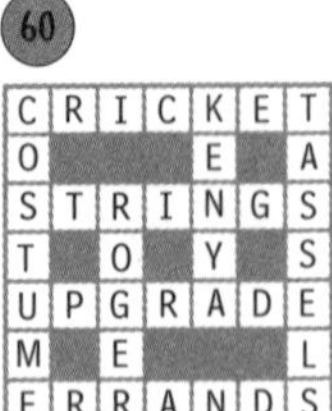

C	R	I	C	K	E	T
O				E		A
S	T	R	I	N	G	S
T		O		Y		S
U	P	G	R	A	D	E
M		E				L
E	R	R	A	N	D	S

61

D	E	C	O	R	A	T	E
R		A		O		I	
E		N	O	B	L	E	S
A	I	D			E		H
M		L			S	E	A
S	P	E	A	R	S		P
	E		L		O		E
G	A	R	L	A	N	D	S

62

T	E	A	L	I	G	H	T
W		R		M			O
E	X	C	E	P	T		M
L		T		S	I	T	H
F	O	I	L		N		A
T		C	O	U	S	I	N
H			N		E		K
	G	I	G	G	L	E	S

63

S	T	O	C	K	I	N	G
	O		A			E	
	P		R	I	O	T	
P	S		R		R		
O			O		A	D	D
N	E	A	T		N		O
D		L			G		G
S	T	I	C	K	E	R	S

64

	W	H	I	S	T	L	E
E		I		A			X
X		F		L	E	A	P
C	O	I	N	S			R
I			E	A	G	L	E
T	O	W	S		L		S
E			T		U		S
D	R	E	S	S	E	S	

65

F	L	U	R	R	I	E	S
R		N		A			A
E	A	S	T	W	O	O	D
E		A			U		N
Z		F			T		E
I	C	E	B	E	R	G	S
N			A		U		S
G	A	I	N	I	N	G	

66

B	L	I	Z	Z	A	R	D
U		T		E			A
L	L	A	M	A	S		R
L		L		L	E	A	K
S	L	I	P		T		N
E		C	O	Y	O	T	E
Y			E		F		S
E	A	R	M	U	F	F	S

67

C	A	L	E	N	D	A	R
O			L		A		I
G	E	C	K	O	S		N
		R			H	U	G
B	O	O			E		
R		W	O	N	D	E	R
E		D		I			A
W	I	S	H	L	I	S	T

68

M	U	S	I	C			
I		A		A	U	N	T
T	R	U	S	T			I
T		C		S	A	N	D
E	V	E	R		R		I
N			O	R	G	A	N
S	O	L	O		U		G
			F	E	E	L	S

69

N	I	C	H	O	L	A	S
O		A			E		T
V		R		F	O	U	R
E	X	T	R	A			A
M			A	T	E		N
B	O	O	M		L	O	G
E		B			S		E
R	E	I	N	D	E	E	R

70

G	E	N	E	R	O	U	S
E		E		A			L
S	L	E	I	G	H		I
T		D		S	O	A	P
U	G	L	Y		H		P
R		E	U	R	O	P	E
E			L		H		R
S	O	M	E	B	O	D	Y

71

D	I	N	G	D	O	N	G
I		E		U			A
S	I	L	E	N	T		T
T		S		E	A	C	H
A	T	O	M		S		E
N		N	E	C	T	A	R
C			A		E		E
E	X	P	L	O	D	E	D

72

M	O	U	N	T	A	I	N
U		R		U			O
S		G	I	B	S	O	N
C	U	E			C		S
U		N			R	U	E
L	I	T	T	L	E		N
A			A		E		S
R	E	S	P	O	N	S	E

73

C	A	S	H	E	W		R
	I		I		A	K	A
B	R	U	T	A	L		N
R		N			N	E	D
A	Y	E			U		O
Z		V	I	C	T	I	M
I	V	E		A		L	
L		N	I	B	B	L	E

74

H	A	Z	E	L	N	U	T
A		I		I			E
R	E	G	I	O	N		S
D		Z		N	E	X	T
S	L	A	M		W		I
H		G	O	V	E	R	N
I			O		S		G
P	E	A	N	U	T	S	

75

S	L	I	P	P	E	R	S
W		D		A			P
E		E		R	E	A	L
A	D	A	P	T			A
T			A	S	H	E	S
E	V	E	R		O		H
R			K		O		E
S	T	R	A	N	D	E	D

76

C	A	R	D	I	G	A	N
A			R		R		E
B	R	E	E	Z	E		I
B			W		W	E	T
A	G	O		W			H
G		P	L	A	I	C	E
E		A		R			R
S	O	L	O	M	O	N	

77

G	R	O	T	T	O		
L			E		U		
A		C	A	C	T	U	S
D	E	A	R		F		I
E		R		D	I	A	L
S	P	I	R	I	T		V
		N		R			E
		G	A	T	H	E	R

78

		F	A	T	H	E	R
		A		A			E
S	U	M	M	I	T		S
E		I		L	E	F	T
C	E	L	L		N		E
R		Y	A	W	N	E	D
E			W		I		
T	H	A	N	K	S		

79

N	A	T	I	V	I	T	Y	
E		A		A		O		
I		M	A	N	G	E	R	
G		E			O		U	
H	I	S	S		T	E	N	T
	T		E			J		I
	S	T	A	B	L	E		G
		A		U		C		E
	B	R	I	G	H	T	E	R

80

G	A	B	R	I	E	L		A
U		E		R		I	N	N
M	O	T	T	O		G		G
		H		N		H		E
H	E	L	P		S	T	A	R
U		E		E		N		
M		H		V	E	I	N	S
A	W	E		E		N		A
N		M	A	N	A	G	E	D

81

		W	R	E	A	T	H	
P		H		V		U		
A	C	E		E	D	G	E	S
L		E		R				P
A	L	L	I	G	A	T	O	R
C				R		A		I
E	E	R	I	E		B	E	G
		I		E		L		S
	S	P	O	N	G	E		

82

H	O	L	L	Y		W		T
A		E		E	N	E	M	Y
R		G		L		P		P
M	I	S	T	L	E	T	O	E
	V						N	
E	Y	E	L	A	S	H	E	S
N		G		N		E		O
V	E	G	A	N		A		B
Y		S		A	T	L	A	S

83

P	E	N	S				N	
L			T	U	R	K	E	Y
A			U		E		W	
T	U	R	F		F	A	S	T
E			F	L	U			W
S	A	R	I		S	A	G	E
	C		N		I			L
D	R	A	G	O	N			V
	E				G	A	M	E

84

P	O	T	A	T	O	E	S	
A		I		A		T		B
R	A	M		R	E	C	U	R
S		E		T				U
N	O	S	E		L	A	W	S
I				L		W		S
P	L	A	C	E		A	T	E
S		R		F		K		L
	R	E	S	T	L	E	S	S

85

L	O	B		S	U	P	E	R
O		A		U		E		O
C	H	A	I	R		A	P	T
K				P		R		
S	U	G	A	R	P	L	U	M
		R		I				E
B	E	E		S	N	A	K	E
E		A		E		I		T
N	O	T	E	D		M	R	S

86

M	O	U	S	E	T	R	A	P
E		F		X		I		I
R	I	O		C		D	U	E
I				U				C
T	E	L	E	S	C	O	P	E
		I		E		U		
A	U	T	O	M	A	T	I	C
R			W	E	D			U
K	I	L	L		S	A	L	T

87

A	T	T	I	C		F	E	W
R				A		I		A
C	O	C	O	N	U	T		T
		O		D		N		E
G	U	M	M	Y	B	E	A	R
R		I		C		S		
I		C	L	A	S	S	E	S
L		A		N				O
L	O	L		E	N	J	O	Y

88

T	U	R	K	I	S	H		
R		A		M		A	C	T
A	P	P	E	A	R	S		R
F		I		G				U
F	U	D	G	E		R	A	F
I		L				A		F
C	R	Y		R	E	B	E	L
	U			U		B		E
	N	O	S	T	R	I	L	S

89

	T	H	A	T	C	H		
	W		W			O	A	F
C	O	M	F	O	R	T		L
U			U			E		U
C	U	R	L		C	L	E	F
K		O			O			F
O		C	H	I	M	N	E	Y
O	A	K			B		Y	
		S	N	O	O	Z	E	

90

	S						H	
C	A	L	F		S	H	O	E
	C		R		I		P	
	K	R	I	N	G	L	E	
			E		H			
	D	A	N	C	I	N	G	
	I		D		N		E	
P	E	T	S		G	O	A	L
	T						R	

91

	J	U	M	B	L	E		
	A			E		A	B	C
C	R	U	E	L		S		L
O				I		E		O
W	E	N	C	E	S	L	A	S
A		O		V				E
R		O		I	C	O	N	S
D	E	N		N			A	
		E	G	G	N	O	G	

92

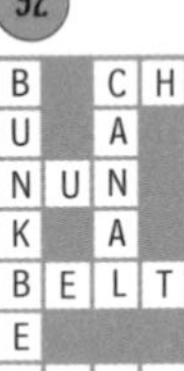

B		C	H	A	R	I	T	Y
U		A		N		O		
N	U	N		T	R	U	M	P
K		A		S				E
B	E	L	T		A	S	I	A
E				P		E		S
D	I	A	N	A		V	I	A
		R		G		E		N
P	A	T	T	E	R	N		T

93

C	I	N	N	A	M	O	N	
L		I			A		O	
O	C	C	U	P	I	E	D	
V		E			D			F
E	A	R	S		S	C	A	R
S			O			H		I
	W	I	N	D	M	I	L	L
	A		G			N		L
	R	O	S	E	M	A	R	Y

94

	N	U	T	M	E	G		
	O		E			O	L	D
S	W	I	M			O		A
T			P	A	R	D	O	N
I			E		E			G
C	I	T	R	U	S			L
K		U			C	U	B	E
S	I	R			U		O	
		N	I	N	E	T	Y	

95

O		L		N	E	V	E	R
B	O	A		O			V	
E		P	A	R	S	L	E	Y
Y		L		T		O		
S	P	A	G	H	E	T	T	I
		N		P		T		R
T	A	D	P	O	L	E		O
	S			L		R	O	N
W	H	A	L	E		Y		S

96

E	L	V	E	S		A	I	M
L		O		U		N		A
M	O	W		B	U	D	D	Y
		E		T				O
P	O	L	A	R	B	E	A	R
A				A		L		
T	O	P	I	C		D	O	T
C		A		T		E		I
H	U	T		S	Y	R	U	P

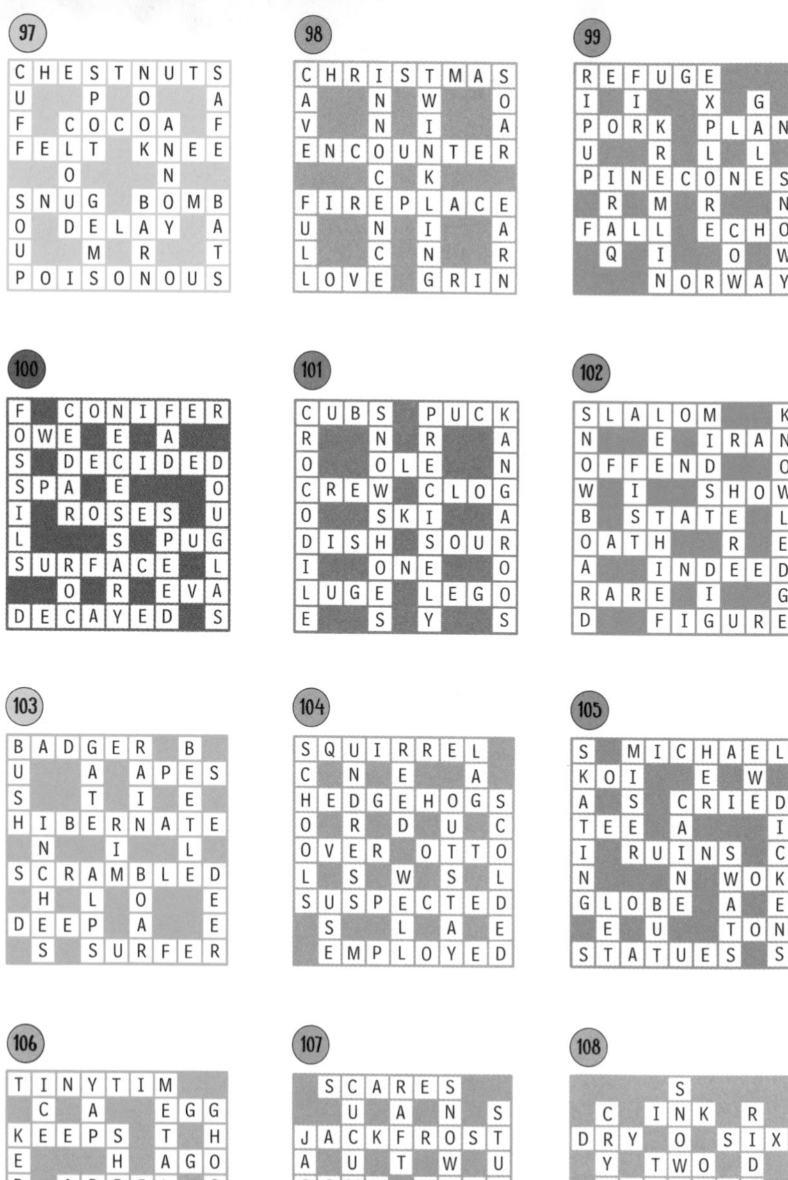
97
CHESTNUTS
U P O A
F COCOA F
FELT KNEE
O N
SNUG BOMB
O DELAY A
U M R T
POISONOUS
98
CHRISTMAS
A N W O
V N I A
ENCOUNTER
C K
FIREPLACE
U N I A
L C N R
LOVE GRIN
99
REFUGE
I I X G
PORK PLAN
U R L L
PINECONES
R M R N
FALL ECHO
Q I O W
NORWAY
100
F CONIFER
OWE E A
S DECIDED
SPA E O
I ROSES U
L S PUG
SURFACE L
O R EVA
DECAYED S
101
CUBS PUCK
R N R A
O OLE N
CREW CLOG
O SKI A
DISH SOUR
I ONE O
LUGE LEGO
E S Y S
102
SLALOM K
N E IRAN
OFFEND O
W I SHOW
B STATE L
OATH R E
A INDEED
RARE I G
D FIGURE
103
BADGER B
U A APES
S T I E
HIBERNATE
N I L
SCRAMBLED
H L O E
DEEP A E
S SURFER
104
SQUIRREL
C N E A
HEDGEHOGS
O R D U C
OVER OTTO
L S W S L
SUSPECTED
S L A E
EMPLOYED
105
S MICHAEL
KOI E W
A S CRIED
TEE A I
I RUINS C
N N WOK
GLOBE A E
E U TON
STATUES S
106
TINYTIM
C A EGG
KEEPS T H
E H AGO
R APRIL S
MAD U T
I O BLESS
TIP A E
TODDLER
107
SCARES
U A N S
JACKFROST
A U T W U
COMB TSAR
K B M T D
EVERYBODY
T R T R
SCHEME
108
S
C INK R
DRY O SIX
Y TWO D
SNIFFED
T ELF L
HAT A NEW
L SKY S
E

109

110

H	U	M		J	E	W	E	L
A		U		A		H		E
R	E	D	R	I	D	I	N	G
S				L		T		
H	O	O	D		B	E	E	F
		R		O				A
R	O	B	I	N	H	O	O	D
U		I		C		I		E
B	A	T	H	E		L	I	D

111

112

L	A	R	A	C	R	O	F	T
A		A		O		U		H
P	A	D		M	A	R	I	O
		I		E				S
S	T	O	P		A	B	L	E
O				W		I		
N	O	R	T	H		R	U	G
I		A		E		D		O
C	O	N	F	E	S	S	E	D

113

114

115

116

First published in 2017 by Usborne Publishing Ltd, 83–85 Saffron Hill, London ECIN 8RT, England.

First published in America 2017